"Like the creeper that girdles the tree trunk,
the Law runneth over and back.
For the strength of the Pack is the Wolf,
and the strength of the Wolf is the Pack."

THE STRENGTH OF THE WOLF IS THE PACK

By SCOTT PETERSON and JOSHUA PRUETT

Based on the screenplay by JUSTIN MARKS

Executive Producers
PETER TOBYANSEN   MOLLY ALLEN   KAREN GILCHRIST

Produced by JON FAVREAU BRIGHAM TAYLOR

Directed by JON FAVREAU

EGMONT

For Catie and Zach; of all the stories in the jungle,
yours will always be my favorite.
—J.P.

For my parents who always believed I could.
—S.P.

EGMONT

We bring stories to life

This edition first published in Great Britain in 2016 by Egmont UK Limited,
The Yellow Building, 1 Nicholas Road, London, W11 4AN
First printed in the United States of America in 2016 by Disney Press,
an imprint of Disney Book Group

Copyright © 2016 Disney Enterprises, Inc.

Book design by Shannon Koss & Scott Piehl

ISBN 978 1 4052 8498 1
66008/2
Printed in the UK

CONTENTS

CONTENTS

PROLOGUE

THE TIGER COULD already taste the boy.

He burned his way through the Jungle, bright hide lighting the brush with flickers of black and orange as he cut through the night.

There was no real fire, no spark of man's Red Flower—not yet—but the fury in his belly could have razed the world. Only one thing could sate his hunger.

The tiger ran on, up and over the trees' great feet that curled their toes into the cold earth. Past the vines that coiled like snakes at his heels, he ran. He thought of his prey with sinister delight. He wanted his prey to be strong, to have fight in it. Easy would be an insult. Easy was not the tiger way.

Tigers have few tales. Some say tigers don't have time for stories. They move too fast, their paws too burdened, their mouths already too full. There's no room for tales on their tongues. But every tiger has one tale: the tale of the hunt. The hunt that lasts a lifetime. The kill that writes the hunter's story in fear and blood.

The tiger was telling his story now. With every leap and bound and stretch of his great shoulders, he told his story. He smiled as he ran, white teeth like shards of moonlight filling his mouth.

Shere Khan hunted the man-cub.

THE **CHASE**

THE MAN-CUB RAN. He scuttled over the Jungle's back, grabbing branch and boulder and hurling himself forward, moving so quickly he was closer to falling, always just catching himself with his next footfall.

Mowgli picked up his pace, barely breathing, his body like the river—moving, bending, twisting but never breaking, surging between trees and over earth, rushing from one moment into the next. He pushed himself faster and faster, the leaves whipping at his face and arms.

The boy was twelve, or as close to that as anyone could figure, and his body was lean and muscled, brown as the bark of the banyan tree and hairless as the crocodile, save for a tuft of unruly black hair atop his head. He had lived in the Jungle all his life, and it showed as he moved like a native animal through the trees.

He leapt and tucked his body, flipping onto a high branch, then heard sudden movement behind him. Instinctively, he leapt off the edge of a great thick tree branch and vaulted from the Jungle canopy.

Mowgli landed in the midst of a pack of young wolves and moved on all fours as the others did. They snapped at him as they sprinted together, then reorganized themselves around Mowgli and ran in a pack, breathing as one, each footfall beating the earth—the music of the hunt, the song of the Jungle.

For an instant, they were a single beast. From behind, the shadow of their pursuer gained ground, and the wolves rushed forward, pushing ahead of the man-cub. Behind them, the cat never faltered, never slowed, its great muscular body built for the hunt.

Mowgli strengthened his resolve, putting more into every move, every lunge, but the wolves were leaving him behind. They were faster, their shorter legs more powerful than Mowgli's.

The creature tracking him was closing the gap. Mowgli couldn't look back. He knew his only hope was to think differently. He could never outrun such a large cat, but maybe he could outthink it. Or, better yet, outclimb it.

Mowgli reached out and grabbed vines as he ran past a large-bellied tree, his momentum swinging him high enough to scramble into the tree's head of branches. There wasn't a moment's hesitation in Mowgli's steps; he moved along the tree as if born to it, narrowly avoiding catastrophe with a simple pivot of his toe or duck of his dark, shaggy-haired head.

Then he was flying again, feet leading, belonging to neither the Earth nor the heavens, before landing on the next outstretched limb, which cried out with a terrible *crack!* The branch beneath him tore away from the tree, falling. And Mowgli fell with it.

The earth spanked Mowgli, the impact of his landing ringing through his limbs. He could hear the predator crashing through the foliage. He tried to run, but it was too late. The cat pounced and was on the man-cub in an instant, pinning him to the cold, dark earth, face close enough to smell his breath. Then it spoke.

"You must be the very worst wolf I have ever seen."

Mowgli pushed the panther off, irritated that Bagheera had caught him once again.

"Yeah, but if that branch didn't break, I woulda made it," protested Mowgli.

Bagheera clawed the belly of the tree, stretching his back, then sat on his hind legs and patted down his fur in places that had been ruffled during their exercise. The great cat was all muscle and reflex, black as night and agile as any creature in the Jungle. If he was tracking you after dusk, you'd see only the glow of his yellow eyes . . . if you saw anything at all.

"Wolves do not hide in trees," said Bagheera. "If you want to live with the wolves, you must live the wolf way."

Suddenly, the Jungle cried out. Yips and calls headed toward them as the young wolves finally circled back to Mowgli and Bagheera. Mowgli lit up as he joined his family, batting and pawing at one another, mouthing one another with safe open jaws.

"How'd we do, Bagheera?" asked one of the youngest.

"Well . . ." Bagheera began, but already the cubs had lost interest.

"Let's go!" barked another. Then they all abruptly broke into a run, Mowgli following them as fast as he was able. He could keep up, but for how long?

The big panther sighed, watching the man-cub trail away into the Jungle.

Such a tale, thought Bagheera. The strange tale of the man-cub called Mowgli.

Bagheera took his worries with him as he padded after his charge, his responsibility, his man-cub, speaking aloud to the forest around him.

"If only the wolf pack needed that man-cub as much as he needed them."

HEADED **HOME**

BAGHEERA FOLLOWED the wolves.

He kept a leisurely pace while remaining mindful
of the Jungle. (Cats can be vigilant with very little
effort; it is in their blood and their eyes and their
twitching whiskers). Bagheera's ears stretched back,
then swiveled forward again, listening, always
listening.

There was rustling in some bushes about three
banyan tree lengths away, but from the titter
accompanying the movement, he knew it was only
muskrats. Behind him rhinos grazed, their signature
sniffles and snuffs and sneezes rising in the midday
air. To his left, he heard birds building nests, another
positive sign. Birds knew trouble on the wind even
before big cats, and the sounds of their normal
routine gave Bagheera comfort.

Several paces ahead, Mowgli, full of youthful energy and vigor, bounced his way home through the Jungle. The man-cub loved the Jungle and always had. Bagheera had fond memories of Mowgli's toddler days, when the bold young man-cub's fearless romps often forced the panther to tackle and hold down the wild child to protect him from himself. But it was much harder for Bagheera to get his paws around him these days. *They grow up so fast,* the panther thought.

"Wolves do not hide in trees," repeated Bagheera, noticing the boy's ever-growing legs and quick-moving knees. Even his stride was growing. A voice inside reminded the cat that the man-cub would need speed one day. For an instant, they were a single beast.

"I wasn't hiding," said Mowgli. "I was evading."

Bagheera laughed.

"You ran up a tree to get away from a panther." He bumped up against Mowgli's waist, almost knocking him over. Even on all fours, the panther stood nearly as tall as the boy, and outweighed him several times over.

"It almost worked, Bagheera!"

"It was a dead tree."

"How was I supposed to know that?" Mowgli picked up a seed and threw it.

Bagheera stopped.

"It had a fig vine. Any tree girdled by a creeper is either dead or close to it."

Mowgli stopped and turned back toward the panther, putting his hands on his hips.

"You just can't say anything nice, can you, old cat?" huffed the boy.

Bagheera shook his head and walked past Mowgli, patience worn leaf-thin. "We have had this conversation so many times I fear I am talking to myself, Man-cub! You must realize that until you can prove yourself, they are never going to let you join their council."

"Yeah, but if that branch didn't break, I woulda been in," Mowgli said, smiling.

Bagheera turned and leapt at Mowgli, putting the man-cub's head in his mouth.

"I think this might make it easier on both of us," said Bagheera. His mouth full, his words were muffled. "It will put both of us out of our misery, and at least one of us will have a full stomach. 'Law of the Jungle,' and all that."

"Stop it!" Mowgli giggled despite himself.
"You're messing up my hair."

Bagheera let go, and Mowgli trotted away.

"You can't do that anymore," Mowgli called over
his shoulder. "I'm not a cub anymore."

Bagheera watched him leave. He knew he was
being hard on the man-cub, but it was a tough
Jungle out there, and it was just going to get
tougher. The only thing that hadn't changed since
Mowgli had first fallen under Bagheera's care was his
basic need of survival. And for that, Mowgli needed
a people. A people to protect him.

THE COUNCIL

MOWGLI DIDN'T THINK he needed anybody.

He could handle things on his own. Well, that wasn't entirely true. But to Mowgli, it seemed everyone was hard on him and never let him do what he wanted to do. Everybody always worried about him, especially Bagheera—Mowgli's shadow.

For as long as Mowgli could remember, Bagheera had been there, always watching, corralling and pushing him like a mother bird picking at her little chick. And he was still doing it.

Mowgli climbed over the hill, making his way to the Wolf Den. He was home! He felt the warmth of the place wash over him, inhaled the familiar smells, took in the sounds of the wolves. Home was like a coat he could slip on, unseen but

always there, comforting him. Mowgli made his
way toward the wolves on the lower level. Dens for
the individual families were made from caves and
crevices, all clustered around a large flat area that was
a playground for the young pups. To Mowgli's left,
the adult wolves climbed the hill to Council Rock, a
great stone dais that tore its way out of the earth and
was the center of all wolf business. At the top of the
rock sat Akela, leader of the wolf pack.

Akela led with his deeds instead of his mouth. He
had fought for his position as head of the pack and
would stay leader until he could fight no longer. He
was tall for a wolf, his thick gray coat unblemished
save for the white tufts at the ends of his paws.

Mowgli knew Akela as a distant father figure,
stern of eye and tooth. The man-cub wasn't sure
if that made Akela a good leader, but the wolves
listened to him, so Mowgli listened, too—mostly.
Akela never approved of Mowgli's "tricks," the little
things the man-cub fashioned from twigs and leaves
and vines, for playing with and for collecting water
from the river. Mowgli knew he shouldn't disobey,
but he couldn't help himself. He thought his tricks
were clever, but Akela made it clear they were

dangerous and certainly *not the wolf way* of doing things.

The boy watched Akela and the Council from the lower level, near Raksha—Mowgli's mother-wolf, his *ami*—as she nursed a young cub. Just being close to Raksha settled Mowgli's restless heart. Raksha was *home* to Mowgli, more than the rock or the Jungle or even the old cat.

Suddenly, Mowgli was covered in swarming wolf cubs. They pounced and played on him with their stubby paws and rough tongues, and Mowgli laughed in spite of himself. Mowgli always wished to be a wolf, to be as strong and as fast as his brothers, but even though he was different, the youngest of the pack never made him feel like anything but family. He didn't know much about where he'd come from before Raksha and Akela took him into their den, but he couldn't imagine life without them there in the Jungle. They were his heart.

The smallest wolf, a runt called Gray, leapt up in a quick darting attack and batted at Mowgli's hair.

"Mowgli, pick us up high!" he said. Mowgli couldn't resist indulging the tiny pup. Gray's boundless energy and enthusiasm were infectious, even if he did act impulsively sometimes. The man-cub playfully scratched the pup behind his dark black ears, the only part of him that didn't sport his namesake gray color.

Mowgli looked at the rock, watching as the older wolves assembled without him. He knew he wasn't welcome there. Not yet. Gray nipped at his fingers, trying to get his attention again.

"How'd it go?" Raksha asked.

"He caught me again," Mowgli replied, wanting to get the words out quickly, hanging his head low.

Raksha moved up to Mowgli, the wolf cubs now nipping at her heels. She softly bumped her head into his.

He butted her back, gently, as she spoke.

"If it is meant to be, it will be," said Raksha, making him feel a bit better.

High above them, Akela stood proud, a giant in the Jungle. He was surrounded by the Council of Wolves. Mowgli didn't know what *council* really meant; he knew those older wolves talked a lot and made decisions about things and told the other wolves what to do and where to go. They scowled often, their faces pulled into frowns. Maybe *council* meant "never smiles."

"Let me hear the Law," said Akela.

The wolves spoke as one, repeating the Law:

"This is the Law of the Jungle,
as old and as true as the sky.
The Wolf that keeps it may prosper,
but the Wolf that breaks it will die."

Mowgli sat, fiddling with dead straw and grass at his feet, mumbling the Law under his breath.

"Like the creeper that girdles the tree trunk,
the Law runneth over and back.
For the strength of the Pack is the Wolf,
and the strength of the Wolf is the Pack."

Mowgli didn't understand some parts of the Law and thought maybe he never would. But saying it made him feel closer to the pack that he wanted so desperately to join.

When the recitation of the Law was done, every wolf in the Seeonee valley turned its snout to the sky and howled, long and loud. Mowgli tried a howl of his own, but it came out weak and strained, as it always did, more of a squeak than a roar.

Near him, Raksha sighed with her whole body, then turned and corralled the little cubs back toward the den.

Mowgli looked at Raksha and thought back to his walk with Bagheera.

Everyone always sighs around me, thought Mowgli. *Why must I inspire such deep breaths from everyone?* The wolf and the panther did their best to raise him, but sometimes he could see in their eyes just how different he was.

Mowgli flexed his toes and lay on his back, looking up at the great arms of the trees above him and the sky beyond those.

He dreamed with his eyes open, thinking about the day when he could be a part of the pack or, better yet, be his own pack. No one would call him man-cub anymore or tell him what to do. He would be his own man, and the Jungle would look up to him. Maybe they would fear him the way they feared Akela.

Mowgli shook that idea out of his head. He didn't want that. He turned over and played with the ants that marched by, feeling large in their small world. Warmed by the sun on his back and soothed by the ants on his fingertips, Mowgli fell asleep in the arms of the Jungle.

THE DRY
SEASON

THE RAINS HAD ceased to fall.

Everywhere the Jungle was changing, color and temperature shifting moods like a hot-tempered rhino. Every creature in the Jungle could feel it, the water leaving them behind as it took to the sky and burrowed into the earth.

The Jungle's usual multicolored hide and vibrant frock turned yellow, then brown and finally black. Along the mighty river, the waters ran to a trickle as all around blossoms shut and withered, the many-petaled eyes of the Jungle closing for a season's sleep, most never to awaken.

Steam rose from the river, the water receded completely, and the breath of the Jungle became stale. The song of the carrion bugs grew louder as the music died in the throats of the birds, who no longer had the voice to croon. Tongues dried and the animals who visited the basin found it diminished to a thin shallow pond.

And standing in the center of the basin was something most had never seen in their lifetimes: the Peace Rock—a long lean ridge of blue stone revealed by the receding waters. For the animals, it was a sign.

At the shore of the basin, the porcupine Ikki was the first to see the Peace Rock, though he was too preoccupied with his property to notice right away.

The porcupine hobbled along, the striped black-and-white quills along his back twinkling in the light as he meticulously attended to the collection of odds and ends the dry season had uncovered as the water had pulled back and away. One by one, Ikki listed each object as he came to it.

"My pebble. My leaf," said Ikki, his pink nose twitching intensely. "No one touches, no one touches. My rock. Two rocks. Three rocks . . ."

Ikki followed the trail of rocks, counting each, until something stopped him in his tiny tracks. He hollered out.

"The Peace Rock! It's the Truce!"

From the other side of the basin, scavengers

gathered to watch, their bellies empty but their mouths full of opinions.

A giant squirrel picked idly at his bright red coat, chewing at the inside of his cheeks. He pointed at the Peace Rock. A pangolin, a pygmy hog, and a hornbill followed his gaze to the stone protruding from the waning river.

"We're all gonna die," said the giant squirrel.

The pangolin licked his plate-armored back with a long dry tongue and then scratched his thin chin, squinting his tiny eyes.

"It's just a rock," said the pangolin. "You see them all day every day. You're standing on one now. I live under one. I look like one. It's just a rock."

"It's a pretty rock," grunted the pygmy hog. He was half-asleep and kept dozing off, leaning against the pangolin to stay upright, his stiff brown bristles poking the few areas of the pangolin that weren't fully armored.

"Squawk," squawked the hornbill.

"The dry season brings the Peace Rock. Peace Rock brings the Truce," said the giant squirrel, who couldn't believe they didn't know this. "Truce brings . . . tourists."

"What are you talking about?" The pangolin asked. "You're telling tales again."

"No, it's true," the giant squirrel said. "Truce means hunting at the riverbank is forbidden. By the Law of the Jungle, drinking comes before eating, so Peace Rock means . . . we aren't gonna die after all. But it is going to get crowded. Which could be worse."

The pangolin moved away and the pygmy hog toppled over, snoring, and stayed asleep.

The hornbill squawked again, the colorful casque over his beak trumpeting his call, then hopped his way across the basin to where the porcupine was collecting his rocks. The hornbill picked at one with a dull yellow claw, and Ikki smacked his beak.

"My rock," said Ikki. "No one touches. The Peace Rock! It's the Truce!"

The hornbill squawked and then lifted into the air on dark black wings as all around him word of the Truce began to spread.

It had been many years since a Water Truce had been called, but the announcement flew from the mouths of deer and wild pig and bison alike, their excitement filling the skies with feathers and calls, wings and words blanketing the Jungle with the news.

WATER **TRUCE**

MOWGLI HAD NEVER seen so many animals.

Never at once and never all in one place. Predators and prey, all drinking from the same small watering hole at the same time.

Raksha led Mowgli, Gray, and the other wolf cubs past the riverbank.

"Wow," Mowgli breathed, amazed. Animals piled almost on top of one another, all vying for a spot, for a chance at what little water was left. In spite of the desperation Mowgli saw in their eyes, and felt in his own stomach, there was something beautiful about it.

Mowgli moved to join the others at the riverside, but Raksha stopped him.

"Do not forget . . ." she said.

"No hunting," said Mowgli, eyes still focused on the animals.

"Playing only," said Raksha.

"Playing only," repeated Mowgli. "I got it, *Ami*."

Raksha moved herself in front of Mowgli, where she could be sure he was paying attention.

"And remember. Not everyone here has seen a man-cub in the Jungle before. So behave yourself."

Then she smiled and said, "Take the pups with you."

They scampered at Mowgli's heels, biting and laughing as he led them to the riverside. They were thrilled.

"Look," whispered Gray. "Nilgai."

"And pygmy hog, and mongoose," added another cub.

Mowgli couldn't believe what he was looking at. A herd of bison bathed in the shallows while brightly colored egrets landed on their backs, using them as perches. A flying squirrel tried to blend in among them, but the bison shrugged it off. Snakes of all shapes and sizes cooled their bodies underwater while turtles stacked atop one another like a rock pile, only inches away. No one seemed to mind or even take notice of how exceptional it all was; they didn't really care. To Mowgli, that just made it all the more amazing. He wondered what the Jungle would be like if its peoples behaved that way all the time.

Deer passed in front of Mowgli and the pups while the bison announced their arrival politely, suggesting those ahead make room for their great girth.

Mowgli watched as a nilgai mother coached her young to the water.

"One after another," she said. "Stay in line."

Suddenly, the new members of the wolf pack, those who had grown from pups to adult wolves, strode past, their heads proudly held high. Mowgli used to run and play with them when they were younger, but now they seemed to exist in a different world.

"Look, the pack!" shouted Gray.

"Hey, guys," said Mowgli to the new pack members, trying to be casual. "What's going on?"

They ignored him. Clearly, not even a Water Truce could bring the man-cub and the wolf pack any closer.

"Whoa," said Gray. "They didn't even say hi."

"They do that to me, too," one of his little sisters admitted.

"That's what happens when they get in the Council," said a third wolf cub.

Nearby, Ikki the porcupine continued to busy himself with his possessions.

"My stick, no one touches."

The porcupine challenged a peacock who came too close to his stick.

"Truce," the bright bird reminded Ikki.

"Truce, yes," repeated Ikki, remembering.

Mowgli smiled as he walked forward, marveling at the small interactions between such different peoples. His fingertips tapped the water pouch tied at his waist, one of his "tricks." Using it, he'd be able to drink from the river as fully as the rest of the pack, even with all those animals crowding the shore.

"Mind the feet," a mongoose said as he crossed the man-cub's path.

Distracted, Mowgli walked right into a rhino drinking at the water's edge. It was like walking into a mountain, and the man-cub was winded for a moment. He stepped back, staring up at the giant creature.

The rhino turned and looked down at Mowgli.

"A man-cub at the drinking place?" asked the rhino. His voice was like the sound of shifting rocks.

The rhino's mate glanced their way.

"That's just Mowgli," she said, a smile on her snout. "He lives with the wolves. Leave him alone. Drink."

She winked at Mowgli, then turned her attention back to the river.

The male rhino flashed Mowgli a skeptical look, then turned back to the water himself. Mowgli exhaled, relieved.

From nearby, the man-cub heard the wolf cubs whispering.

"Rats," said one.

"Let's get 'em!" said another.

The cubs chased a group of rats beside the shore. Mowgli joined the fun, cornering the small rodents. They turned their small mouths up to the man-cub and squeaked nervously.

"Water Truce," they said. "Water Truce."

The cubs moved in for the attack anyway but froze instantly at the sound of an angry hiss to their left—a cobra. It rose up to full height, its bejeweled hood level with the man-cub's soft, unprotected neck.

Mowgli and the cubs recoiled. The cobra hissed again as the rats scurried away. The cubs were terrified.

"Wa—water Truce," they stammered. "Water Truce!"

The cobra slithered away. Mowgli and the cubs turned to one another, relieved. Then they burst out laughing.

As time passed, more and more creatures gathered at what was left of the watering hole. Soon Bagheera arrived, wading through the gathered peoples of the Seeonee to drink.

It was a full house, more than the old cat could ever remember gathering that way before.

Mowgli's water pouch bobbed past the panther and the others, inviting looks from many bewildered animals. It was fashioned from a discarded pelt and lashed together with vines so it would hold water, if only temporarily. A longer length of vine pulled it along the river. Mowgli, perched on a rock above the water, reeled it in, proud of what he had made.

Some of the other adults stared uneasily at Mowgli and his invention. A curious nilgai calf moved to get a closer look but was stopped by its mother.

"Stay here," she warned.

Mowgli offered some water to Gray, who sat at his side, then sipped victoriously. Feeling mischievous, Mowgli spit water between his teeth at the youngest wolves on the Council as they drank at the river below. Gray laughed, eating it up. Suddenly, there was a growl behind Mowgli.

"Drop it," said Akela.

Mowgli turned and saw the head of the pack standing over him. Mowgli did as he was asked.

"What did I say about your tricks?" asked Akela.

Mowgli knew from his tone that it wasn't really a question, but felt like he should answer just the same.

"But, Akela, I couldn't get . . ."

"What did I say?" repeated the wolf.

"It's not the wolf way," conceded Mowgli.

"No more tricks," said Akela. The wolf moved away, and Mowgli sighed. He dropped to all fours and sulked back to the riverbank. Mowgli didn't understand. He knew it wasn't the wolf way, but that didn't mean it was *bad*. Mowgli's trick worked! He had figured out a way to get *more* water from the river *faster*. Surely that must count for something. But it didn't—not in Akela's eyes. It made Mowgli feel distant from the pack, different, like he was alone even though he was surrounded by his wolf brothers and sisters.

Bagheera watched all this with a full heart. He knew Akela to be stern, yes, but he also knew that Akela was merely trying to protect the man-cub.

Others joined in as Akela watched the river. Suddenly, the wind changed and the sky grew darker. Akela's hackles rose ever so slightly. Bagheera lifted his head, noticing the vultures flying above. His entire posture shifted, muscles tightening, ears back. Something was wrong.

A young buck froze midgulp, mouth hanging open. He stared, terrified, at a shadowy shape on top of a nearby rock. One by one, all the peoples at the river stopped and lifted their eyes. Bagheera rose on his haunches and growled.

Mowgli looked up. Bagheera never growled. The man-cub followed the panther's gaze to the rock where the Bengal tiger sat. His fur was bright with black stripes, elegant but for the old burns scarring his coat.

It was Shere Khan.

SHERE KHAN

THE TIGER LICKED his lips and smiled at the buffet before him.

Every people, every *meal* of the Jungle was there at the river's edge. His mouth watered.

He watched as the wolf cubs were herded behind the adults.

Raksha motioned for Mowgli to join them.

"Behind me," she said, never taking her eyes off the tiger.

"What is it?" asked Mowgli.

"Not another word."

Mowgli ducked behind Raksha but peered out, fascinated. How could one animal have such an effect on so many others?

The tiger dropped down from his perch and took a slow lap around the Peace Rock.

"Please," he said. "Don't let me interrupt."

Every eye was on Shere Khan; every creature withdrew in fear as he sauntered past. Snakes slithered away, and tortoises popped their heads back into the safety of their shells. The great tiger stepped on one of Ikki's sticks, and the porcupine trembled.

Shere Khan was massive. His thick muscles rolled and flexed under his beautiful striped hide; he was a creature built for one thing and one thing only: killing.

He took a long slow sniff of the air, eyes closed, enjoying himself. Mowgli was surprised how joyful the tiger seemed for a creature that instilled so much fear.

"I just love a hot summer night," said the tiger. "All the fragrances in the air. All the stories the wind carries."

He stopped by the river and drank in absolute silence. No one breathed.

"Everyone comes to the Peace Rock," the tiger continued, licking his chin and flicking his whiskers. "So many smells to catch up on."

He sniffed the air again.

"But I . . ."

He stopped. He sniffed the air a third, then a fourth time.

"I can't help but notice, there's this strange odor tonight. What is it, this scent I'm on?"

Shere Khan made his way slowly to the wolves. Mowgli felt Raksha pull him closer.

The tiger shifted his gaze over the wolves, then found Mowgli with his bright amber eyes.

"I'd almost think it was some kind of . . . *man-cub.* . . ."

"Mowgli is spoken for, Shere Khan," said Akela firmly. Mowgli was amazed. The wolf seemed utterly fearless in the face of this much larger animal.

" 'Mowgli,' " said the amused tiger. "They've given it a name."

The man-cub was confused. Why was this animal so interested in him? He felt a tinge of fear.

The tiger turned to the gathered peoples.

"I apologize if I'm slow. I'm just a simple tiger. I'm not a complicated kind of beast. But when was it we came to adopt man in this Jungle?"

"He's just a cub," said Akela.

Shere Khan leaned closer to the wolf, the burns in his fur more pronounced as he drew nearer. Mowgli thought he looked more like a monster than a tiger.

"Does my face not remind you what a grown man can do?"

Akela didn't respond, so the tiger turned to address the peoples of the Jungle again.

"Shift your hunting grounds for a few years and everyone forgets how the Law works." The tiger spoke with a smile, but there was no joy in his voice. "Well, let me remind you: a man-cub becomes *man*, and man is forbidden."

Raksha shifted on her paws, hackles raised. She spoke under her breath.

"What do you know about Law?"

"Raksha," warned Akela.

But she would not be silenced.

"Hunting for pleasure. Killing for power. You've never known Law."

Shere Khan paused, danger in his eyes, but Raksha wouldn't back down.

"The cub is mine," said Raksha. "Mine to me. So go back where you came from, *burned beast*."

There was a long moment when no one moved or breathed, Shere Khan simply staring at brave Raksha, Mowgli's *ami*. Then Akela growled.

"Raksha. Enough."

Akela—powerful, unyielding—rose atop the rock and called out.

"The tiger knows who rules this part of the Jungle. I am sure he does not intend to come here and make threats. Especially during the Water Truce."

The other wolves rose with Akela, taking aggressive postures that Mowgli recognized. A show of force. Shere Khan glared at them. The gathered peoples waited for things to escalate, but instead the tiger spoke again.

"I am deeply respectful of these laws that keep us safe. So here is my promise. . . ." He crossed in front of the Peace Rock. "Nothing lasts forever. The rains will return and the river will rise. And when that rock disappears, this Truce will end."

Shere Khan looked back through the crowd and locked eyes with Mowgli.

"You want to protect him? You claim him yours? Fine. But ask yourselves: how many lives is a man-cub worth?"

And just as suddenly as he'd come, the tiger was gone again. Mowgli stood in confusion. *What is this all about?* Bagheera watched the man-cub, concern on his face and in his heart.

Many of the animals bristled uneasily, both hoping for rain and dreading its return.

The tiger was gone, but the sky growled with his lingering threat.

RAINS of CHANGE

THE TIGER'S WORDS tore at Mowgli's head. *How many lives is a man-cub worth?* What had he meant by that?

Mowgli turned the threat over in his mind and his heart as the rains returned. When he was growing up, the clouds' breaking and pouring their waters back into the earth was a reason to celebrate. But now that Shere Khan had left the mark of his words on the Jungle, everything had become quiet and dark, and even the birds seemed to lose their voices.

The wolves argued for many days at Council Rock, faces low and full of frowns, with Bagheera, observer and advisor, nearby in an adjacent tree. Gray and Mowgli watched from afar, catching pieces of the adult arguments and the occasional angry growl. Mowgli could hear Raksha over the rest.

"What are they talking about?" asked Gray.

Mowgli just stared. Simple questions didn't seem to have simple answers anymore.

The tiger wanted him dead, but why? Surely there was other food in the Jungle for a cat that big. If not, then Mowgli knew the pack was the only thing that stood between him and Shere Khan's belly. As the Council argued, some shared their love for Mowgli, while other, older wolves expressed a worry that they'd be risking war with the fearsome tiger by protecting the man-cub. He knew he was not of the wolf pack, not really, but he'd spent his entire life hoping to become one of them, and now they debated his worth, the value of his life, without ever truly acknowledging his place among them. Mowgli felt like he was a burden to the pack, and maybe that was all he'd ever been. As the Council spoke, Mowgli couldn't hear all their words, but what he did catch tied knots in his belly and pulled at his heart. They barked and growled for days, until one cold night, Mowgli had heard enough. Sick with questions he couldn't ask, Mowgli saw Raksha making a final appeal to the Council. He knew what he had to do.

"He cares for the cubs," pleaded Raksha. "He pulls thorns from our paws. He is part of the pack. The strength of the wolf is the pack."

His *ami*'s speaking the oath caused the other wolves to grunt and bare their teeth. Mowgli moved closer to their gathering, quiet and unseen.

"Even the strength of the pack is no match for the tiger!" barked a wolf lieutenant, his face scarred by old wars.

The man-cub looked to Raksha, who shook her shoulders and raised her ears. She didn't back down. Mowgli had never seen her so upset.

"We raised him as one of our own. Why should that change now?"

"Because Shere Khan will kill him," countered the lieutenant. "And kill all who try to protect him!"

"Enough." Akela spoke, silencing them both. "This is my decision."

Everyone turned to Akela, whose voice was serious but not mean. Mowgli saw warmth in his old eyes.

"We always knew that someday he would have to leave us. But we are the only family he has ever known. If he stays, we must be prepared to give our lives." Mowgli's heart tore at the inside of his chest. He had to say something; this was *his* story, not theirs.

Akela moved to speak again, but Mowgli rose from his hiding spot and stood. He planted his feet firmly and spoke up for himself, his voice shaking under the weight of his words.

"Then I'll leave!" exclaimed Mowgli.

The man-cub strode into the middle of the Council. The circle of wolves parted, surprised. Bagheera sat up on his haunches on the tree branch.

"Mowgli. Go back to the den," said Raksha. Her tone was tense, sharp.

Mowgli summoned every ounce of courage he could and defied her. He needed to be heard. His hands shook as he spoke, so he closed them into fists at his sides.

"That fixes it, right? I can hide in the Jungle, and the tiger won't bother you anymore. . . ."

Akela looked into Mowgli's eyes, firm.

"This is not for you to decide."

Mowgli stood his ground, staring right back at Akela. Determined. The warmth in the old wolf's eyes was gone, replaced with a flicker of something else, but Mowgli didn't care. This was no "trick," no plaything they were debating. This was Mowgli's life, and he would have his say, even if it meant disobeying the only family he'd ever known. He would not let them put their lives in jeopardy because of him.

Then Bagheera dropped down and entered the circle.

"Akela," said the panther, "perhaps I can be of help."

The other wolves turned, taken aback by his interruption. Mowgli wasn't sure what the old cat would do or say, but his next words almost knocked the man-cub over.

"The boy is right," continued Bagheera. "Maybe it is time he found another place."

Bagheera was actually *agreeing* with him.

"No," said Raksha. She stared past Bagheera, catching Akela's gaze.

Bagheera continued: "I am the one who brought him to you. And now I shall return him to where he belongs. . . ."

That wasn't exactly what Mowgli had intended, not really, but before he could say anything himself, Raksha turned on Bagheera, her ears back, ferocity in her words.

"I will not let you. He is my cub."

Akela looked at Mowgli, the warmth back in his eyes.

"It is the only place he'll be safe," Akela said. Then he turned to Bagheera. "You have my decision, old cat."

Raksha gritted her teeth and closed her eyes. Mowgli looked to his mother-wolf.

"It's okay, *Ami*," said Mowgli, his voice soft. "I won't go far. I'll come back and visit."

Raksha walked up to her man-cub and placed her head against his. Mowgli was overcome with emotion and memories. The familiar smell of her coat put pictures in his head, behind his eyes. Mowgli small, very small, grabbing at Raksha, pulling her snout as she licked his face, cleaning him. Sleeping on her warm fur, feeding and listening to the low hum of her wolf song. Running with her, learning to forage. All those past seasons were a jumble in Mowgli's heart and mind, and they caught in his throat. The only constant in his life was those wolves, his family, and he was choosing to leave them. It felt so wrong, but Mowgli knew he couldn't stay. Staying meant putting his family, *his pack*, in danger. He had to go.

"Never forget this," said Raksha. "You are mine. Mine to me. No matter where you go or what they may call you. You will always be my Mowgli."

Her words broke something in Mowgli, and his eyes ran wet with water like a warm rain.

The man-cub looked up at Akela and saw that flicker in his eye once more. But now Mowgli realized it was something good. Was it respect? Pride? A combination of the two? Mowgli's vision blurred, and overwhelmed, he turned his back on the wolf.

Bagheera led Mowgli away, and the pack watched the man-cub leave for the last time. Gray called after Mowgli, barking, howling for his brother, but Mowgli didn't answer; he couldn't. Gray howled until exhaustion stole his voice from him. As one, Raksha, Akela, and the others took up the call, some of them howling until the dawn came, howling for their man-cub.

THE JOURNEY HOME

MOWGLI WAS LOOKING for a new family.

"The turtles like me," mused Mowgli. "I could stay with them. Or the rhinos? They always let me hang around. Of course, the rhinos sleep standing up. I don't think I'd be very good at that. I don't know, which do you think is better?"

"Neither," said Bagheera, never breaking his stride.

"What about bears?" Mowgli suggested. "They live in caves just like the wolf pack. Maybe I could—"

"You do not want to get involved with bears. Trust me."

"I guess I could live with the birds. I do like it in the trees, but all that chirping and tweeting

and squawking and on and on and on . . . I think it
would drive me nuts. All that racket. They never
stop."

"I cannot imagine what that would be like,"
Bagheera said dryly. "But I am not taking you to
join any of those packs."

"What do you mean?"

"I am bringing you to the Man-village,
Man-cub."

"What? Bagheera, I don't know *man*."

"You will," said the cat. He walked with his tail
low. Mowgli pawed at it as they traveled.

"But, Bagheera, you always said: 'You're not
supposed to go near a Man-village.'" Mowgli
changed the timbre of his voice and mimicked
Bagheera, drawing out his vowels and turning up his
nose.

Bagheera pulled his tail out of Mowgli's hands
as they crossed a restless stream into an even denser
part of the Jungle, great trees reaching high into the
mists.

"That was different." Then he thought a moment
and added, "I do not sound like that."

"Why is it different? You always said, 'Stay away
'cause you might fall in a trap or get eaten or get

hurt by flying rocks or other things that could get you killed.'"

"I know what I said," snapped the old cat, but then, suddenly, he stopped short.

At their feet, pebbles trembled, then rolled, then leapt off the ground. Deep rumbling rocked the Jungle floor like an earthquake.

Giant forms, almost too large to be real, emerged from the mists. Like moving granite walls, they passed—regal, self-possessed, and fearful of nothing. Their powerful trunks, bigger than the man-cub, swayed gently between jutting ivory tusks.

Elephants.

Mowgli's mouth dropped open as the majestic giants moved in somber procession. It was beautiful.

"Whoa," said Mowgli.

Bagheera, his head lowered, whispered at Mowgli through clenched teeth.

"Bow your head!"

"Why?"

"Show them respect."

Mowgli took a knee beside the old cat, keeping his head down and stealing glimpses as the elephants marched on without acknowledging the man-cub or his panther escort.

Once they were gone, Bagheera lifted his head and continued his lecture.

"The elephants created all that belongs in the Jungle. The rivers, the trees, the birds in the trees. But they did not create you, so that is why you must go."

Bagheera strode ahead, Mowgli trailing behind.

"What if I lived with the big cats?" asked Mowgli.

The odd pair moved farther into the Jungle, the old cat leaving a trail of sighs behind them.

THE PANTHER grew impatient.

Mowgli and Bagheera had finally reached an embankment at the edge of the Jungle, where the high grasses began. Bison grazed here and there, a chorus of lowing and chewing rising on the afternoon breeze.

"What if I lived with the nilgai?" Mowgli asked.

"No."

"Or the mongoose."

"This is not a discussion."

They dropped into the field, the tall grass brushing their bodies.

"Bagheera, this is my home. I don't even know what man's like."

"You'll learn."

"But I want to stay in the Jungle. Why do I have to be somewhere else?"

Bagheera stopped and turned.

"Because the Jungle is no longer safe for you, Mowgli."

Mowgli put his hands on his hips.

"Was it ever?"

Bagheera was done. He looked Mowgli in the eye, speaking slowly and emphatically.

"You are being hunted. By a tiger!"

Bagheera turned back to the trail and led the way.

"Only man can protect you now."

The man-cub noticed a hint of disappointment in the old cat's voice, and it hurt. Back at the Council, the old cat had actually said Mowgli was right, something he'd never done before. It had made Mowgli feel good, made him feel older, responsible, *big*. But now, out here, it was back to the same old cat, the cat who always knew better no matter what. Mowgli's *shadow*. Mowgli was done living in the panther's shade.

"Bagheera, this isn't fair."

Bagheera didn't respond. He was far more focused on their environment, eyes scanning for danger, ears moving, listening. Always listening. A

porcupine burrowed into his den at the edge of the
tall grass, and a kite flitted from tree to tree above
them. Quiet—almost too quiet.

Bagheera forged on cautiously.

Mowgli continued to plead his case. "You're not
even giving me a choice. And there's a lot of stuff
you're not telling me, too. Don't think I don't notice."

Bagheera slowed to a stop. Something was
wrong. The bison fell silent, and the wind died
down. The only sound in the Jungle was Mowgli.

"You say you're taking me where I came from,
but you found me in the Jungle. Are you bringing
me back to the Jungle? No. Why are you bringing
me to the Man-village if you found me in the
Jungle? And why does the tiger hate me so much,
anyway? Does he even know me? It sure seems like
he knows me. . . ."

"Down," said Bagheera.

"What? Now we have to bow to the bison, too?"

Bagheera's tone changed, and his jaw tensed.

"Listen to me. This is not a game. When my ears
go back, you are going to run to that ravine."

Mowgli looked ahead, seeing the spot past the
grass.

"What are you talking about?" asked Mowgli.

"Go to the north," said Bagheera, "where the sky glows at night. I will find you on that path."

Mowgli grew impatient.

"Bagheera, I'm not taking one more step until you tell me what—"

The man-cub never finished his sentence.

In a blur of fur and fury, a figure leapt out of the tall grass.

Mowgli froze.

Bagheera snarled and met Shere Khan in midair.

They collided, titans of the Jungle, and fell struggling and thrashing into the grass. The bison, spooked, scattered in every direction.

And for once in his life, Mowgli did what he was told.

He ran.

As the snarling adversaries landed, Shere Khan rounded and launched another fierce attack, but Bagheera dodged, rebounded, and struck back. His talons tore across the tiger's flank, opening a large gash that would have given a lesser opponent reason to flee, but Shere Khan was not about to back down.

The menacing demon sprang forward, throwing his full weight at the smaller cat and knocking him off his feet to tumble across the ground, locked in a deadly embrace. They carved into the grass around them, kicking up mud and snapping reeds as they battled.

Bagheera fought valiantly against the much larger opponent, but Shere Khan was relentless, striking again and again until, finally, the tiger caught Bagheera with a sharp claw across the face and threw him down. Shere Khan turned and sprinted after his man-cub.

Bagheera lifted his head, trying to stand, but he was too weak and collapsed.

There was a clap of thunder, and a bolt of lightning illuminated the Jungle as a long-awaited storm broke, the sky rupturing and spilling forth rain like blood from a wound.

At the edge of the tall grass, Mowgli ran for his very life, the tiger on his heels. Mowgli knew he'd never outrun Shere Khan, but he couldn't give up, not now, not ever. The hulking beast raced toward Mowgli and closed what little space there was between them, the wet grass parting in his wake. It was over.

Then the bison stampede slammed into Shere Khan, knocking the tiger sprawling into the reeds. Mowgli kept moving, narrowly avoiding the thrashing river of panicked bison himself, dropping, slipping, and sliding down the muddy hillside and into the wet ravine.

Mowgli had barely a moment to catch his breath before the bison piled into the ravine after him, covering him with mud. He was running with the herd, trying to keep up, when he noticed, just behind, the dirty orange-and-black flash of Shere Khan on the ridge above. They locked eyes for a moment through the downpour, Mowgli finally seeing the heat in the tiger's predatory glare. The hatred.

And just as quickly, the stampeding creatures came between them, blocking their view, and Mowgli lost sight of Shere Khan.

The tiger sprinted this way and that, hunting, leaping, chasing bison in every direction, but found nothing. His man-cub had disappeared. He roared, splitting the sky with his fury, his cry competing with the thunder for supremacy.

This was far from over.

THE JUNGLE swallowed Mowgli.

The rains had returned with a vengeance, turning the strong earth into shifting mud, and the family of bison Mowgli huddled against slipped and slid along the slowly sinking ridge. He hid among their hairy bodies, clinging to their backs, wet and exhausted.

The trees shouted at him as he passed, their cracking trunks rattling the air around them like snapping jaws. Mowgli looked up in time to see the mighty banyans falling down in great patches and clumps, as if something almost impossibly huge was pushing its way through the Jungle toward them. More and more towering trees fell as the unseen animal moved closer and closer.

Then the monster felling the trees revealed itself as the Jungle belched a monumental wave of mud;

there was no great animal, only a moving mountain
of wet earth racing their way. It exploded through
the tree line, leaving the Jungle broken in its wake.
It was what the elders called a mud slide. Mowgli
had never seen one with his own eyes, had only
heard the stories. It was worse than he could have
imagined and it was headed his way.

One sweeping arm of the mud slide blocked their
path going forward, scattering the frightened bison.
The creature Mowgli rode backed away in terror,
struggling hopelessly to find sure footing as the mud
rose to cover its legs. Then, from behind, another
stream of mud, like a tail, whipped the fleeing bison
off their feet entirely.

Before he could react, Mowgli and the bison
were pushed down the mountain by the angry
brown river of choking mud and broken trees. Its
eyeless face smothered Mowgli. Splinters and rocks,
like the teeth of a giant, bit at his back and arms as
he tumbled. Over and over again, he tried to plant
his feet, but the ground was moving too quickly
beneath him. Mowgli was carried faster than he had
ever moved in his life, at the mercy of the twisting,
churning mud flow.

Suddenly, the canopy of trees overhead was gone and there was gray sky in front of Mowgli. The Jungle had opened to reveal a cliff, and the man-cub, the bison, and the shattered trees were swept over the edge and into the swollen river.

Animal and brush and rock rolled in the current and under the water, Mowgli with them. The river roared in his ears and in his nose and mouth, trying to bury him with its fury. Mowgli reached out, scrambling, eyes wide and desperate. He grabbed wildly and felt the wet hair of a bison, and then it was ripped away from him by the water. The man-cub struggled to keep his head above the surface, a losing battle, until miraculously his hands found the splintered body of a tree branch. He hugged it close, even as the churning, roiling current dragged them both under the water and into the darkness.

After what seemed like an eternity, Mowgli and the log broke the face of the river.

Mowgli gasped as the large branch he clutched nearly lurched out of his hands, careening down the spine of the river, bucking Mowgli up and down as the rocks below churned the water this way and that, hurling the man-cub farther and farther downriver.

Mowgli held on for his life with what little strength he had left.

The gray sky towered angrily over the Jungle, spilling water from the clouds, bearing down on Mowgli as he was pushed deeper into the Jungle than he had ever been before.

Gradually, eventually, the downpour lessened, the rough river calmed, and the water from above and below grew quiet. The rain stopped and the river slowed and Mowgli felt the log come to a stop, the sounds of the shore creeping into his ears. It was a long time before Mowgli opened his eyes. But when he did, he didn't recognize anything.

Mowgli didn't dare move, still clinging firmly to the tree limb. Only his eyes moved, darting back and forth, looking, searching, trying to find something familiar. He was terrified of what else could be in such a dark corner of the Jungle. He was still wet but now with sweat and fear. He'd never been so afraid in his life, and it bloomed in little beads of water all over his body. Sounds, strange and new, called out to Mowgli. It was the first time the man-cub had felt truly alone.

He had been bold, had tried to do what was right for his family, but it hadn't worked the way he had hoped. This was much, much worse. Like a nightmare he couldn't wake from. No wolf pack, no cubs, no Bagheera, no Raksha.

And now not even the Jungle wanted him.

THE **NIGHTMARE JUNGLE**

MOWGLI COULDN'T TELL if he was awake or asleep.

He blinked, then shut his eyes as hard as he could. When he opened them again, nothing had changed.

The Jungle is not right *here,* he thought.

After he'd climbed off the broken tree limb, it had sunk back into the river. Now Mowgli felt small on the strange shore. The air was thick and wet and gray and he could almost touch it. He passed his hands through the fog, and it moved like floating water, then disappeared. All around him, animals cried and the trees audibly ached, stretching their limbs in the wind. Shadows moved behind the brush, then vanished as if they'd never been there at all.

Mowgli stumbled around the Jungle, not sure of

a single step. He was too tired to run but too scared
to sleep. He was lost. He called out the name of the
one animal he wanted to see, hoping the old cat was
okay and close by.

"Bagheera? *Bagheera?*" said Mowgli. "Come on,
Bagheera . . . where are you?"

Suddenly, Mowgli heard something in the brush
nearby. It was close. Too close.

Mowgli spun in place, squinting hard in the mist.
Then he saw movement in the trees. More moving
shadows. Thin but frightening. He couldn't quite tell
what they were.

But as Mowgli's eyes adjusted to the light he
started to make out horrifying images. Fierce
glowing eyes. Jagged yellow teeth. In the dark, in
the rain, in a part of the Jungle where the man-cub
was a stranger, these creatures seemed menacing.
Everything seemed menacing.

Mowgli dove under a tree stump. A lump grew
in his throat and a burn boiled in his belly. He was
sweating again.

Mowgli could feel that something was still there.
Silent. Then more rustling. He waited, hiding,
barely breathing.

When it finally grew quiet again, Mowgli swallowed the fear and looked out of his hiding spot. The trees were empty.

The creatures were gone, but Mowgli wasn't relieved. If anything, he was more scared than before.

Mowgli ran.

Wet leaves slapped his arms and face, but he didn't care. He just had to get away. He ran blind. Mowgli didn't know how long he could run or how far; he was quickly growing tired. Tired of being beaten up by the Jungle, tired of being hunted. He needed help.

"Bagheera!" cried Mowgli.

He waited. No one answered.

Soon he grew too fatigued to run farther. There was no one to help him. He was utterly alone. He dropped his head, as close to despair as he'd ever been.

At his feet, Mowgli noticed something. He squatted on his haunches and spread his toes wide to support his weight. His arms hung to the ground, hands picking at the flaky and see-through *skin* someone had left behind.

Mowgli stood and held it up, stretching it wide between his arms. The skin sagged low, his arms not long enough to stretch it all the way out. Whoever had shed it, thought Mowgli, was huge. He dropped it suddenly, growing nervous again. He backed away.

A grumbling in Mowgli's stomach turned his mind to more pressing matters. He realized he hadn't eaten since he had left the Wolf Den, and home or no home, he had to find food sooner rather than later.

Searching the ground and surrounding foliage, Mowgli noticed creeper vines choking a tree in their embrace and found they were covered in figs.

Mowgli used a vine to make a loop and with the loop tamed the branch, pulling it down. Once it bent low enough, Mowgli could grab the figs comfortably, and he did, filling his mouth.

But again there came the sound of movement.

Mowgli almost choked. He spun around to face his "visitor." At first, he feared it was the shadow creatures again or, worse, whatever had shed that skin, but he quickly saw there was no reason to be alarmed.

This was no hunter, no monster. This was only a silly little furry creature barely bigger than a squirrel—a civet. It was brown with white markings, its bushy tail waving and its pink nose twitching as it whistled at Mowgli through the small gap in its teeth.

There was a part of Mowgli that wanted to cheer and howl and jump for joy at seeing the little animal. He hadn't realized how lonely he'd become.

"Oh," said Mowgli, smiling. "Hey there."

The little civet turned its head to the side.

"Do you have a language?"

The civet put its paws to its mouth, making a motion like it was eating or wanted to eat.

Of course, thought Mowgli. *The little guy must be hungry, too.*

Mowgli grabbed a fig and held it out for the animal. "Wanna share?"

The civet nibbled at it, swallowed, then nodded.

"You're welcome," said Mowgli.

The man-cub watched as the civet licked its paws and smoothed its fur, putting on a show. Mowgli chuckled at the little rascal, not noticing that over a dozen other mischievous civets were at work behind him, using the distraction to steal the rest of Mowgli's figs.

Then a branch snapped and Mowgli spun around, catching them in the act.

"Hey!"

They squealed and scattered, taking the fruit with them. Mowgli chased them up a branch and into the trees, but they scrambled away, just out of reach.

"Hey," said Mowgli. "Those are mine!"

Suddenly, the civets were gone, disappearing as quickly as they'd come, almost as if they'd been spooked. Mowgli was left alone up the tall tree, surrounded by silence and mist.

"But I'm still hungry," he said to no one. He sighed, contemplating how to get more to eat.

Suddenly, a vine slithered along a higher branch behind Mowgli.

Mowgli turned but saw nothing in the mist.

"Hello?"

From nearby, there came a strange sound, like hairless hide scraping ever so slowly across tree bark. Mowgli could feel his heart beating hard.

"Who's out there? I'm all out of figs!"

Suddenly, a slow, smooth voice cut lightly through the mist.

"I'm not here for figs, little cub."

Behind Mowgli, something huge shifted. The man-cub turned and his breath drained from his chest as he watched an unimaginably massive python uncoil from above, its giant head pushing through the air directly toward him.

THE **VOICE** OF
THE **SNAKE**

MOWGLI COULDN'T BREATHE.

The python moved closer and Mowgli tried
to scoot away, but there was nowhere to go. The
creature was literally all around him; its intricately
scaled body stretched from one branch to the next
to the next, encircling the entire area. Mowgli
shivered as he realized he couldn't even see where the
python's slowly undulating body ended.

"Oh, no," said the snake. "Don't be scared. I'm
not going to hurt you."

The snake's voice was sweet. It reminded Mowgli
of honey for the ears. Against all reason, he relaxed a
little, and his eyelids suddenly felt heavy. He shook
his head to clear it. Something about the voice of the
snake made Mowgli sleepy.

"I was just passing through," said Mowgli. "I don't want any trouble."

"There's no trouble," said the snake. Her beautiful eyes stayed locked on Mowgli's. "Are you alone out here? That's not good. We should never be alone."

Mowgli hugged himself, his fear moving his body reflexively.

"I'm, uh, waiting for my friend," said Mowgli. "He shouldn't be too long now." Mowgli tried to mask his alarm, but that only made it more obvious. He wasn't sure, but the more uncomfortable he got, the more pleased the snake seemed, a small smile curling up the corners of her large mouth.

"I can stay here with you. Until he gets here."

The snake moved closer and Mowgli shrank deeper into his own skin.

"Would that be all right?" asked the snake.

"Please, I—I . . ." stammered Mowgli.

The snake's head stopped swaying, hovering directly in front of the man-cub's face, her eyes dancing in front of his, changing shape, color shifting like the sky at night—only faster, much faster. Mowgli felt dizzy and warm.

"I'll keep you safe," she said, her tone darker now. "Just you and me, sweet thing."

"Who are you?" mumbled Mowgli. There was hardly a question in his voice at all; his fear was being replaced by that sleepy feeling again.

"Kaa . . ." said the snake, exhaling her own name like a razor-sharp whisper, tongue cutting the air quick enough to leave a scar in the mist.

Kaa the snake coiled closer to Mowgli, her scales bristling in anticipation.

"Poor, sweet little cub. What are you doing so deep in the Jungle?"

Mowgli's head was swimming.

"This is my home," said Mowgli. The words came but only barely, falling from his lips as if he'd forgotten how to speak.

"Don't you know what you are?" asked Kaa. "I know what you are. I know where you came from."

"You do?"

"Yes," said Kaa. "Would you like to see?"

The snake put her forehead to Mowgli's. All the man-cub could see were Kaa's eyes, spinning and flashing; there was no place else to look.

"Yes," said Mowgli.

Mowgli felt his body tumbling forward without ever moving, falling down and down and down into the eyes of the snake.

THE DREAM

MOWGLI NO LONGER saw with his own eyes.

Where once he had seen the Jungle, now he saw only blackness, and out of the darkness winked stars. And a trail of gray clouds leading to a cave. But the clouds were odd and small. Not clouds at all. They were *smoke*.

Mowgli heard Kaa's voice in his head. "Mostly men stay in their village—far from the dark of the Jungle."

Mowgli moved closer to the pictures that hung behind his eyes. He watched the smoke rise from the cave, its mouth glowing red. It felt like a dream, but Mowgli thought he was awake.

"But sometimes they travel," continued Kaa. "And when they do, their caves breathe in the dark."

Mowgli could see better now and he noticed the smoke rising not from the cave but from a circle of wood on the ground. Suddenly, he was there, not just looking at it, but standing near the bright, hot glowing circle. Drawn to it.

"They call it the Red Flower," said Kaa, her voice louder now, closer. "Fire. Man's creation. It brings warmth, and light, and destruction to all that it touches."

Just then, a man's shadow moved within the cave. Mowgli froze, fascinated, then whispered to the snake in his head.

"Who is that?"

"A traveler, protecting his cub."

Behind Mowgli, two amber eyes burned in the shadows of the brush—the eyes of Shere Khan. There was a roar and the tiger leapt past Mowgli and into the cave.

Mowgli shuddered. Shere Khan, there, in that place? Was nowhere safe?

The man-cub watched the shadows of the man and the tiger grapple. The man wielded a stick of wood, fire dancing from the tip, and he struck the tiger with it. Mowgli watched as the tiger became one with the Red Flower, howling and roaring in pain, the flower's red-and-orange petals growing and licking at the dark night, driving Shere Khan into the Jungle, blinking out of sight.

"Shere Khan ended the man's life that night," continued Kaa. "But not before he was burned by the Red Flower's touch. He ran so fast he didn't notice the cub he'd left behind. . . ."

Mowgli stared at the cave, noticing a crying man-cub, much smaller than Mowgli, barely more than a babe, for the first time.

"And that cub was you."

He couldn't believe what he was looking at.

"Me?"

Suddenly, there was a stirring behind the little Mowgli. Out of the dark stepped the night on four legs: a panther.

"Bagheera," whispered Mowgli.

Bagheera stared at the tiny man-cub, then approached, cautious. The little one stopped crying and reached out to the panther. He grabbed the panther's nose and squeezed. Bagheera sneezed and the little man-cub giggled.

"The panther found you," said Kaa, "but he couldn't change what you would become."

Mowgli watched the scene shift and burn as

the flames from the cave grew and grew, until they obscured his view of anything else.

And there, standing wrapped in the Red Flower like a second skin, Mowgli saw himself. Older, harder, wearing a face that hadn't smiled in seasons. Behind that fearsome Mowgli, the Jungle burned like the tiger.

"The man-cub becomes man. And man brings destruction to all."

Mowgli closed his eyes, but the images wouldn't leave.

"That's not me. . . ."

"Oh, you poor sweet thing."

Mowgli tried to fight the lure of the snake's voice, but the harder he struggled, the less he could fight. His chest felt tight, like a great hand was squeezing him. Mowgli tried to take a breath and found himself back in the Jungle, *his* Jungle, and the snake had wrapped him tightly in her coils. He was trapped.

But strangely, Mowgli wasn't worried, wasn't afraid. He knew it was wrong, but the snake made him feel so relaxed, so sleepy, he stopped fighting. He again had the feeling he was falling without moving, and then he could feel Kaa's breath on his face.

As she spoke, every word gently blew the hair off Mowgli's forehead.

"You want to stay here," said Kaa.

"Yes," said Mowgli. He was smiling.

"You can be with me if you want. I'll keep you close."

Kaa's eyes turned deep black, and her mouth opened wide.

"Let go of your fear now. Trussst in me. . . ."

Kaa lifted and tightened her coils, her scales brushing against Mowgli's chin as she constricted more tightly around the man-cub. She opened her mouth wider still, unhinging her jaw on both sides, her tongue licking Mowgli's face.

Suddenly, there was a great roar and a huge dark shape lunged out of the Jungle and threw itself on Kaa. With no time to strike, the great snake hissed and released Mowgli, who fell and landed in the dirt, waking from the living nightmare she had trapped him in.

Mowgli looked up in time to see Kaa rear back and hiss at the huge shadow looming over her. The great beast stood on its hind legs, roared again, and threw its huge hairy frame onto the lowest hanging loop of the snake's endless body, pulling her from her perch.

That was the last thing Mowgli saw before he passed out in the mud.

THE **FALL** OF
COUNCIL
ROCK

THE NIGHT WAS STILL, but Raksha's heart was not.

She lay with her litter, one eye on them as they played outside her den, another eye on Akela and the other wolves up on Council Rock. She was unsettled. Somewhere out there was another piece of her family, one of her own, whom she could not see, and it made her restless, eating at her insides like a bug.

A small commotion, just outside her line of sight, snapped Raksha from her melancholy. It was Gray. It was always Gray, wasn't it? He was off on his own and he had something in his mouth.

"Gray, what's wrong?" asked Raksha. "Why are you not playing with the others? What is that you have?"

Gray sauntered over to his mother and dropped the object at her paws; it was Mowgli's water pouch. Raksha's muzzle fell, her emotions overtaking her strong face. Gray looked up.

"Why did he have to leave?" he asked.

Raksha closed her eyes.

"Gray . . ."

"We could have protected him. We shouldn't have let him go."

Raksha put her forehead against Gray's and pushed gently.

"I miss him, too," she said. "The important thing is that he is safe now."

Gray pulled away, seeing something moving out of the brush behind his mother. His little mouth quivered and he dropped his head. Raksha turned, immediately on guard. All the members of the wolf pack rose to their feet, instantly alert, as Shere Khan confidently marched in.

Without turning her eyes from the tiger, Raksha spoke to her cub.

"Get inside."

Gray moved quickly back into the den with his brothers and sisters.

Raksha watched, never blinking, as Shere Khan strode silently past the gathered wolf pack and all the way up to Council Rock, where Akela was waiting.

"Yes?" said Akela.

Shere Khan cracked a small smile, one of his great canines peeking past his lip.

"I suppose you know why I've come."

Akela nodded, calm and strong. Raksha looked up and saw vultures circling overhead. They followed the tiger wherever he went. *Disgusting creatures.*

"The man-cub is no longer here," said Akela.

Shere Khan chuffed in his throat and shook his head just so.

"I thought I made myself clear," said the tiger. "I wanted him turned over to me."

Akela moved toward Shere Khan.

"We no longer harbor him. He has left the pack."

Raksha looked to Akela then, knowing that saying those words hurt him nearly as much as it hurt her to hear them.

"And where, may I ask, has he gone?"

Shere Khan still sounded amused, but his posture told an entirely different story. Raksha could read the angle of his shoulder blades and the position of his back paws. He was getting ready to move, and move quickly.

The leader of the pack spoke deliberately. "The Man-village," Akela said. "He is with his people now."

"So, the man has left the Jungle," Shere Khan drawled.

"Yes. You and I no longer have a quarrel, and most importantly," said Akela, tilting his head down to address Shere Khan more directly, "we have peace."

"Well," said the tiger, "I guess it's done, then."

And just like that, Shere Khan leapt down and took three steps away. Raksha could sense Akela and the others relax, but something wouldn't allow her to do the same.

"Unless I can draw him back out . . ."

Suddenly, Shere Khan spun and launched his great body at Akela. The wolf leapt to his feet to defend himself, but it was already too late; the tiger was too fast. The sheer force of the larger animal knocked the wolf back against a rocky ledge, slamming his head into solid stone. Taking no chances, the tiger lunged at the wolf's exposed throat. Raksha looked on in horror, and before she, or anyone else, could lift a paw, her mate, the father of her cubs, was dead in the tiger's jaws. Their entire world had changed in less than a heartbeat.

The pack watched, frozen, as Shere Khan dropped Akela over the edge of Council Rock. His lifeless body plummeted to the cold, hard ground below and the vultures quickly seized the moment, diving for their feast.

All around Raksha the other wolves retreated to their caves, scattering to hide and mourn. The fear was palpable. Raksha could taste it, but she still didn't move. She watched the tiger, an impostor standing atop Council Rock, now red with Akela's blood, clean his teeth with his tongue and address her people.

"HAVE I GOT YOUR ATTENTION NOW?" roared the tiger. "I didn't want it to be this way. I made it so simple. All I asked was for one thing, and you denied me."

Raksha stared at the tiger, feeling the presence of her cubs in the den behind her, a fury burning in her breast and legs and teeth.

"Well, that ends now," continued Shere Khan. "Spread the word: until I have the man-cub, these hills are my hills. You didn't respond to reason; now you will know fear."

The tiger lay down, satisfied, and began to clean his coat, his giant pink tongue lifting the red stain from his hide.

In the midst of her torment and rage, Raksha's thoughts turned to Mowgli. She was glad he had not been there to witness Shere Khan's savagery, and hoped beyond hope that he was safe.

THE BEAR

INSIDE THE DARK, a sliver of light found Mowgli's face.

It crept slowly and warmly over his cheek and up to his eye, waking him. Mowgli sat up, his left hand bracing him as he wiped his eye with the meat of his right. He turned his head side to side, trying to make out his surroundings—a cave.

Mowgli jumped to a crouch, balls of his feet planted firm, ready to move at a moment's notice. His finely tuned senses waited for a subtle shift in the shadows or a tiny noise in the dark. What he did hear was weird, like a bird calling from the belly of a tree.

The man-cub barely had time to register just how strange that warbling was before he caught sight of movement just to his right; there was something in the cave with Mowgli. Something big and furry. Something that was chewing.

Then Mowgli's stomach growled, loud and gurgly, giving away his position.

The chewing sound stopped suddenly and a big furry paw came out of the shadows into the light, offering a berry branch.

It was a bear—a bear easily six times Mowgli's size.

"Hey there," said the bear, his mouth full. "Hungry?"

Mowgli yelled and leapt backward against the cave wall, legs kicking at the floor.

The gargantuan bear was a mottled brown and very heavy, though it was hard to tell what was fur and what was bear beneath his great coat. His warm brown eyes looked out intelligently across a long black snout, one smeared with liberal amounts of berry juice. He didn't seem to mind. He pulled back the berry branch he had offered to his visitor and looked it over, running it under his dark wet nose, inspecting it, hunting for some clue to explain Mowgli's extreme reaction.

"Get away from me!" hollered Mowgli.

"So it talks. How about that?" said the bear,

who'd gone back to eating. He seemed much more interested in the food than in the man-cub. Once he was done picking the branch clean of anything edible, the bear lazily turned his body and put his large nose in Mowgli's face.

Without thinking, Mowgli smacked the bear on the nose.

"Ow," hooted the bear, rubbing his face.

"You better not eat me," warned Mowgli, trying to scale the cave wall. He climbed and clambered, but it was useless. Mowgli slumped down onto his haunches, keeping his arms up just in case the bear tried to get close again.

"I'm not gonna eat you, kid," said the bear. "I don't eat monkeys."

"I'm not a monkey," Mowgli said, offended.

The bear scratched his chest, raising his brow. "You're not?"

"No," said Mowgli, standing up.

"Oh. Well, you look like a monkey," said the bear.

Faster than he should have been able to, the bear moved closer to Mowgli again, backing him all the way up against the cave wall, sniffing at him.

"Long arms, little tuft of hair," said the bear.

Then he took a big sniff and scrunched up his nose, cringing. "Oooh, you sure smell like a monkey."

"What is wrong with you?"

Mowgli pushed the bear away and quickly slipped under his arm and into another corner of the cave.

"Hey, hey, settle down, would you, kid?" said the bear. "There's no need to get all worked up."

"Where am I?" demanded Mowgli.

"My cave. Lucky for you," said the bear. He stared at Mowgli for a moment.

Mowgli scowled back at him. "What?"

"Don't you remember what happened?" asked the bear.

Mowgli crossed his arms. *Are all bears this dumb?* he thought. "No . . ."

The bear smiled proudly, closing his eyes.

"Well, I saved your life, that's what," said the bear. "Snatched you right outta the jaws of death!"

The bear moved his giant clawed paws in the air as he told his story.

"Or coils of death was maybe more like it. That python had you all wrapped up, son. Lucky for you, ol' Baloo was passing by."

The bear put his paws on his hips and pushed out his chest.

"Who's Baloo?" asked Mowgli.

"He's the bear," explained Baloo, deflating instantly. "I mean, me, Baloo is me. I'm Baloo."

Baloo the bear produced another berry branch seemingly out of nowhere and offered it to Mowgli.

"You sure you're not hungry?" asked the bear. "These berries are tasty enough to make a grown bear weep."

"No!" said Mowgli. He folded his arms and kicked the branch away.

Suddenly, the bear sat up straighter, mouth hanging open. He snatched the branch back and held it close to his chest.

"Hey, monkey," said Baloo. "There's no need to be rude. . . ."

"I told you, I am not a monkey!" said Mowgli, standing.

"Fine, you're not a monkey," said Baloo, chewing. "And neither am I last time I checked. No monkeys in the house. Okay? Just tell me this. Can you climb?"

Mowgli scrunched up his nose at the bear.

"Yeah," said Mowgli. "I can climb."

Baloo got to his feet and made his way out of the cave. Mowgli moved out of his path.

"Good," said Baloo. "Then let's stop wasting time and get to it."

"Get to what?" asked Mowgli.

Baloo turned and smiled, his giant teeth gleaming in the low light.

"Payback, kid. Payback."

PAYBACK

IT OCCURRED to Mowgli that Bagheera probably wouldn't approve of his spending time with this big lazy bear, and that helped Mowgli make up his mind rather quickly.

As fast as his little legs could carry him, Mowgli was following Baloo into the Jungle, which was buzzing and breathing, drinking in the morning as it woke.

Mowgli took two steps for every one of the bear's, enjoying the sights around him. Picking the occasional berry from the packed bushes as he passed them, he could hear a river mumbling quietly nearby. Sunlight bounced from leaf to blossom and back again, filling the air with pollen and color.

"What do you mean, 'payback'?" asked Mowgli.

"Payback for what?" He wiped his juice-covered chin with the back of his hand.

"The Third Law of the Jungle clearly states that when someone helps you," explained Baloo, who was still chewing berries, "you gotta help them back."

In front of them stood a great cliff, rising high above their heads and blocking out the morning light. Baloo walked right up to the cliff face and stuck his paw against a trail of moisture coming down the rock. When he pulled his paw back, it was covered in honey.

Baloo licked the liquid in great goopy gulps. His closed eyelids fluttered and the corners of his mouth turned up.

Mowgli licked his lips. He hadn't had honey since he was very small. He put his hand in the honey trail, pulled it right back out, and licked his fingertips.

The man-cub was starting to enjoy all the eating that came along with being in this bear's company.

"I never heard that law before," said Mowgli.

"Well, now you have, so pay attention," said Baloo, licking his lips. "You see this lovely golden honey? Now if you look way, way up, there's a whole stash of this. Right there. And there. And there."

Baloo pointed his dripping paw as he spoke, up toward the top of the cliff.

Mowgli craned his head up. Up and up. Then higher. And higher, till his neck was sore. At the very top of the cliff was a large crack in the wall. And in and out of the crack flew enormous bees. As soon as he saw them, he could hear them buzzing as if they were in his head, the sound of their fast-beating wings flowing down the cliff with the river of honey.

Baloo stepped back, putting his paws on his hips. Then he sat down with an ungraceful plop and scratched at his chin. Mowgli could smell the sweet honey still on the bear's breath.

"So all I need you to do is shimmy on up there and get me some of it."

Mowgli's face dropped.

"You're kidding me."

Baloo closed his eyes, lowered his head, and placed a paw to his chest.

"Ordinarily, I'd do it myself . . ." said the bear.

"You saved my life so I could steal you some honey?"

Baloo smiled.

"Something like that, yeah."

"No way," said Mowgli.

Suddenly, Baloo was on his feet again. He really could move fast. When he wanted to, anyway.

"Why not?" asked Baloo. "You can do it. I know you can."

"No, I can't," said Mowgli. "Not without . . ."

Mowgli hesitated, his thoughts drifting back to Akela, Raksha, and Bagheera. They had told him not to.

"Not without what?" pressed Baloo.

Mowgli sighed.

"Not without my tricks," he admitted. "I'm not supposed to use them in the Jungle."

Baloo grabbed the sides of Mowgli's head, almost laughing as he spoke. "What? That's crazy! If you've got tricks, use 'em! That's what I say!"

Mowgli pulled away from Baloo's paws.

"I can't."

Or could he? Mowgli felt torn inside. Like a vine that had been pulled in too many directions. He walked away from Baloo.

Even out there, so far from home and those who had always told him what to do, his life was *still* determined by their rules and laws. Everywhere he went it was their Jungle, and never his. They told his story for him, stealing it from his mouth and his heart.

Baloo followed the man-cub, almost running to catch up.

"Kid, try to understand. I'm a bear," said Baloo, "which means I've gotta eat my weight every day for, uh, um, hibernation purposes. . . ."

Baloo had seemed to lose his tongue, but it was enough to make Mowgli pause mid-mope.

He turned and looked at the bear.

Baloo stepped closer, lowering his large head again but keeping his eyes on Mowgli's.

"Look, I know I'm asking for a lot," pleaded Baloo, "but I really need your help. Winter's coming."

Baloo patted his large belly.

"I'm not gonna make it, kid," said Baloo, making his bottom lip quiver as best he could. "Whattaya say?"

Mowgli looked from Baloo to the bees high in the cliff, then back to the bear. The man-cub considered. Maybe it was time to start telling his own story.

TRICKS

MOWGLI WAS MAKING something.

Baloo tried to peek over the kid's shoulder to get a better look, shifting back and forth quickly from foot to foot, but Mowgli moved to block his view.

"How much longer is this gonna take?" asked the bear.

Baloo's stomach grumbled. Loudly. Birds in nearby trees were startled by the sound and took to the air.

"You want your honey or not?" asked Mowgli.

"I do, but can't you pick it up a little? I'm starving."

Mowgli moved again, turning to reveal a group of vines he had braided together to make one longer, thicker vine. Baloo had never seen anything like it before.

" 'Starving'? You just ate all those berries," said Mowgli.

"I got a fast metabolism," said the bear.

Mowgli pulled a tree branch from its trunk, snapping it clean away, and began fashioning some kind of weapon with it. To Baloo, it looked like a long tooth, one end pointed and serious.

"Hey, kid. I hate to keep bringing this up, but I did save your life."

Mowgli threw the length of wrapped vines over his shoulder and across his chest. He planted his tooth-stick in the ground and cocked his hip.

"I'm ready," said Mowgli.

"What is all that?" asked Baloo.

"Don't worry about it," said Mowgli.

"You need any help?"

"Nope," said Mowgli. "Just stay out of my way."

Mowgli marched past the bear, determined.

"That I can do, little brother," said Baloo, smiling a bit. "That I can do."

Baloo saw that something about the little monkey-not-a-monkey had changed. Something he couldn't quite put his paw on, but he liked it.

Mowgli was a spider, dangling from a handmade silk line.

The rope he'd fashioned from vines was working. He'd been nervous at first, but with one end of the rope around his arm, the other end tied firmly to a tree above, and his spear attached to his back, Mowgli had gone from scared to thrilled. His trick was working.

He lowered himself from the top of the cliff until he was level with the first opening in the cliff side and he could see the honeycomb. He used his feet to maneuver against the rock face, stepping cautiously and keeping a careful distance from the humming honeybees. Mowgli looked down and saw Baloo.

The man-cub knew what he was doing was very dangerous; it was a long way down and the honeycomb was well guarded, but none of that bothered the bear, who was too busy scratching his huge bottom against the nearest tree to worry. Mowgli was doing all the work for him.

"You're doing great, kid!" said Baloo. "Far as I can tell, anyway. . . ."

"There's a hive up here, all right." Mowgli grimaced as a rather large bee buzzed by, inspecting him before quickly moving along.

Baloo made satisfied growls as he leaned against another tree and scratched his back up and down.

"Describe it for me," said Baloo, licking his lips. "Talk slow. Don't leave anything out."

"Well," said Mowgli, "there's a lotta bees here. . . ."

Another two bees flew past Mowgli's ears. Then a third. They were getting more curious about their new visitor. Mowgli felt sweat break out on his brow.

"Don't worry," said Baloo. "They don't sting."

"Ow!" said Mowgli. A bee had stung him.

"Except the females. They sting. A lot."

Mowgli decided he'd better hurry this along. He took his spear and poked the honeycomb, swatting at it and the bees that were now circling him.

Below, some scavengers trotted out of the foliage and made their way toward Baloo, the hornbill leading the way, squawking at nothing in particular. The pangolin and the giant squirrel padded behind.

They squinted at the monkey hanging from the vine and poking at the honeycomb in the cliff.

"Hey, Baloo," said the pangolin, unsuccessfully attempting to scratch himself with his exceedingly short claw.

"Hey, fellas," said Baloo, not taking his eyes from Mowgli.

"Who's the monkey?" asked the giant squirrel.

"Man-cub," corrected Baloo. "I'm, uh, training him."

Mowgli was stung again, hard. He instinctively recoiled, losing his balance. He slipped, howled, then grabbed hold of his vine rope just in time.

"Looks like you got your work cut out for you," observed the pangolin.

"Yeah?" Baloo scowled at the pangolin. "Looks like you got a pointy face, so mind your own beeswax and let me tend to mine."

"Okay, Mr. Sensitive . . ." said the pangolin, half curling into a ball.

Above, Mowgli was swinging in the air and making war with the bees.

"Ow. Ow. Ow," said Mowgli. The bees were winning.

The hornbill landed on a branch near Mowgli and squawked loudly.

Mowgli swung at him with the stick.

"Get away, noisy bird! Ow! Ow!" said Mowgli, getting stung a few more times.

"Everything okay up there?" asked Baloo from below.

"I'm—ow—getting—ow—stung—*ow!*"

"That sounds about right," said the giant squirrel.

"Stay with it, kid!" hollered Baloo. "Don't let that get you down!"

"Down is right," added the giant squirrel.

Mowgli ignored them and the bees, using his toes to grab the edge of the cliff where the honeycomb was waiting. He pulled tight on the vine rope and arched his back, slowly straining his body forward over the edge and onto the relative safety of the ledge. He let go of the rope, stood up on the ledge, and was instantly swarmed by bees.

Baloo watched as the man-cub swatted at the bees, turned, and almost fell backward off the ledge.

"Oooooh," said the scavengers in unison.

Baloo scoffed. Those jokers were worse than vultures.

"I can't watch," said the pangolin, curling all the way into his defensive ball.

Baloo moved forward, arms out. He might have to catch the kid.

Mowgli grabbed the ledge, saving himself, legs kicking free below.

"You got it, kid!" said Baloo. "Believe in yourself!"

The pangolin peeked out of his ball and squinted at Baloo curiously. Baloo shrugged. He had just said the first thing that came to his mouth. He was hoping it'd be enough.

From the nearby brush, the pygmy hog ambled toward the scavengers.

"What's happening?" the pygmy hog asked.

"Man-cub's gonna fall off a cliff," said the giant squirrel. He pointed up at Mowgli, who was still struggling to keep his grasp.

"No he ain't," said Baloo.

"Cool," said the pygmy hog, sitting down to watch the show. The scavengers passed some seeds and nuts around, chewing absentmindedly as they watched, never taking their eyes off the man-cub.

Finally, Mowgli managed to swing his long legs up and over the ledge and pull himself to safety.

Baloo sighed out loud, relieved.

"Kid's gonna put me in an early grave," he said to himself.

"There you go!" he called out to Mowgli, his paws on the sides of his mouth.

On the ledge, Mowgli climbed up on top of the honeycomb, one hand still on the vine rope, and jumped up and down on the treat while trying to keep as many of the bees away as possible. Even from Baloo's vantage point, it was getting more intense by the moment.

"Kid's got a death wish," said the giant squirrel.

There was a great snapping sound and suddenly the honeycomb broke free from the cliff. Down it went, and Mowgli with it, losing his grip on the vine.

For a moment, both man-cub and honeycomb were flying.

Baloo moved quickly, trying to guess where the kid would land. He put his arms up and out, ready for anything.

The hornbill squawked and the pangolin came out of his ball. The giant squirrel covered the pangolin's eyes with his paw.

Mowgli reached out and grabbed the vine,

swinging into the canopy of trees as the honeycomb fell past him.

"Here it comes!" hollered Mowgli.

The honeycomb headed straight for Baloo.

"Sweet mother," said the bear just as the honeycomb landed right on top of him.

The scavengers observed Baloo, suddenly the strangest-looking but happiest animal in the Jungle: part honeycomb, part bear. Baloo was bathed in honey, slurping it off his fur and his paws and nose.

"Ha!" laughed Baloo. "How about that, fellas? He did it! He did it!"

"I gotta get me a monkey," said the giant squirrel.

"Man-cub," corrected the pangolin.

"I gotta get me a man-cub," said the giant squirrel.

"Oh, yeah," added the pygmy hog.

"Squawk," squawked the hornbill.

Nearby, Mowgli lowered himself to the ground from the vine. He wiped the last of the bees off his shoulders, then caught sight of Baloo in all his honey-gulping glory. Mowgli smiled. *Silly bear,* he thought.

"Okay," said Mowgli, dusting off his hands, careful to avoid the swelling bee stings. As far as he was concerned, he'd done his duty and now he had to follow through on the agreement he'd made with Bagheera. "We're even now. Good-bye."

Mowgli marched off, but Baloo was on his feet almost instantly, following the man-cub, the honeycomb breaking apart on his coat as he moved faster than he'd moved in many moons.

His meal ticket was leaving him behind.

THE BARGAIN

"WELL, HOLD ON A MINUTE. What's your name, anyway?"

Baloo was not about to let a find like this man-cub slip through his fingers without a fight.

Mowgli kept walking but answered. "Mowgli."

Baloo picked up his pace to keep up, dancing from one side of Mowgli to the other as they both walked, leaving the other animals behind. The hornbill squawked, but no one cared. The show was over and the scavengers headed back into the Jungle.

"Mowgli!" said Baloo. "Terrific name. I like that name. Look, I got a lot more gathering to do in these next few weeks . . . a *lot* a lot, on account of my hibernation and all . . . and I could really use the help. Especially from someone with such clever tricks."

Baloo smiled the biggest smile he could and a bee flew out of his mouth.

Mowgli kept walking.

Baloo caught right back up.

"Maybe you stick around and we split shares," offered Baloo. "Proportional to body weight, of course . . ."

Mowgli didn't skip a step as he spoke. "No way. I'm not getting stung again just so you can eat. Anyway, I can't. I have to go to a Man-village."

"A Man-village? Why d'you wanna go there?"

"I don't," said Mowgli.

"First sensible thing you've said today—" Baloo started, but Mowgli cut him off.

"But I don't have a choice. There's a tiger hunting me."

"A tiger? Why?" asked Baloo.

"Because I'm a man-cub, all right?" Mowgli said, stomping. "Just leave me alone."

"Hey, hey, hey, Mowgli. Buddy."

Baloo placed a soft paw on Mowgli's shoulder. There was honey still on it and it stuck a bit.

"Sorry," said the bear. "What's wrong with being a man-cub? Being a man-cub is great!"

Finally, Mowgli stopped. Baloo couldn't think

and walk at the same time anymore, so he sat down. What was going on with this kid?

"It is?" asked Mowgli.

"Of course it is!" said Baloo. "It's who you are. And that's the best thing you can be. Yourself. You get what I'm saying?"

"I guess," said Mowgli.

Baloo scooted over and put his big arm around Mowgli's shoulder, encouraging the man-cub to sit next to him.

"Look here, Mowgli. I'm just gonna lay this on the line. I like you. You know why?"

Mowgli shook his head.

"'Cause you got something I don't see much around these parts. It's called potential."

Mowgli tried the word on his tongue, weighing it as he spoke.

"'Potential'. . . ." He didn't know what it meant.

Baloo got excited and stood up, flapping his great big paws around like giant bird wings.

"That's right. And there is nothing worse than a cub, a man-cub, who doesn't live up to his potential. Mmm-mmmm. That's a darn shame is what it is. But I'm tellin' you, you don't have to go to some Man-village to be a man."

Mowgli's mind spun. Could this bear be right?

"You can be a man right here in the Jungle. And lucky for you, I'm just the bear who can help you do it!"

Mowgli's eyes grew wide, a smile drawing across his face as he thought of the possibilities, and then, suddenly, the smile was gone. Baloo watched the kid age five seasons right before his eyes. It broke his big bear heart to see it. The burden the kid carried was weighing him down plenty.

"I can't," said Mowgli. "I gotta get moving. Bagheera told me—"

Baloo almost shouted. "Bagheera! Hah!"

"You know him?" asked Mowgli, perking up a bit.

"Oh, do I know him," said Baloo, shaking his head. *Poor kid has been brainwashed by that uptight old cat. No wonder he's so messed up.*

"You know what that cat's problem is?" offered Baloo. "C'mon, I can think of six or seven without even breakin' a sweat." But he didn't wait for Mowgli to answer. "I'll tell you his problem. He always plays by the rules! Always. And sometimes rules were meant to be broken!"

Mowgli had heard enough. It was too tempting an offer and if he stayed a moment longer, he knew he'd make another mistake, do something stupid, stick his hand in another honeycomb. There was honey with this bear, but there were also bees. Lots of bees. He'd learned that much.

Mowgli got up to leave.

"Well, he told me to go to the Man-village, so that's where I'm gonna go," said Mowgli, throwing up his words like a pangolin shell to cover his heart.

Baloo jogged in front of Mowgli, craning his great head down so he could stare the man-cub right in the eyes.

"You're makin' me run, kid. Nobody makes me run. Tell you what—you wanna see a Man-village? How about ol' Baloo takes you there?" offered the bear. "I'll show you a Man-village. Then you, man-cub of the Jungle, then you can decide for yourself. Deal?"

Baloo put out a big paw, honey drying between his clawed fingers.

Maybe the bear is right. Maybe Bagheera is wrong. Maybe—

Mowgli thought for a moment, his heart filling

right back up with hope, and the promise of a new story, his own story, pushing Bagheera out of his head with a rush of emotion.

He stuck out two hands and shook Baloo's paw up and down.

"Deal," said Mowgli.

UP THE
MOUNTAIN

THE BEAR AND THE MAN-CUB cut
through the belly of the Jungle.

Dwarfed by the gargantuan twisted branches of
the thousand-year-old trees reaching high to blot out
the sun, Baloo and Mowgli clambered up the steep
overgrown trail. Few animals used it any longer, but
the man-cub had no trouble keeping up as the bear
huffed and puffed his way higher. Mowgli laughed.

"What?" asked Baloo. "You got a funny to share,
share it."

"You sound like a snorting rhino," Mowgli said,
laughing again. *"Hrumph hrumph hrumph!"*

"I said if you had a *funny* to share it. It's hard
work being this beautiful. And I have a bit more me
to carry up this hill than you do, little man-cub."

"A *lot* more," Mowgli agreed, running quick circles around the lumbering bear.

Eventually, the path flattened out and Baloo's puffing eased. He hummed to himself as he walked. Soon he was singing.

"Look for the bare necessities, the simple bare necessities. Forget about your worries and your strife. . . ."

"What are you doing?" Mowgli asked, his brow knitted as he stared at Baloo. He had never heard such strange sounds from a ground-dwelling creature. From the birds in the sky, perhaps, but never from a bear.

"It's a song," Baloo replied, "about the good life."

"A song?" Mowgli repeated, puzzling over the word. "What's a song?"

"What? You never heard a song before? Didn't the wolves ever sing?" Baloo stopped in his tracks, astonished.

"I don't know," Mowgli said, struggling to remember. "We howl and . . . Oh! We say the Law of the Jungle!"

Mowgli stood at attention, reciting from memory, his voice serious and monotone: "This is the Law of the Jungle, as old and as true as the sky. The Wolf that keeps it may prosper, but the Wolf that breaks it will die."

"Kid, that's not a song," Baloo groaned, shaking his head. "That's propaganda."

Baloo pushed through the brush, past the confused man-cub, muttering under his breath. "That kid doesn't have a poetic bone in his body."

As the two climbed higher, Mowgli found himself falling behind. The man-cub refused to admit he was tired, but in time his heavy breathing gave him away.

"Now who sounds like a rhino?" Baloo chuckled.

"My legs are shorter than yours," Mowgli grumbled. "I have to take a lot more steps."

"All right, all right," Baloo sighed, stooping down to Mowgli's level. "Climb on." With a smile and a whoop, Mowgli leapt nimbly onto the broad downy back of the mighty bear, grabbing fistfuls of fur to hold on tight. Baloo grunted and began lumbering up the hill.

"Kid, I don't know what kind of hold you got on me, but let me tell you I wouldn't do this for just anybody. Doing extra work—heck, doing *any* work—well, that's just not in my nature."

But despite the extra effort, Baloo didn't stop, and the two continued to rise up the twisting spine of the mountain.

Up the mountain trail they climbed, the air growing thinner as they broke free of the thick Jungle canopy, its familiar sounds and smells giving way to the gentle breath of the wind and a new scent that Mowgli did not recognize.

Mowgli climbed down from Baloo and gasped, taking in the view before them. The vastness of the mighty Jungle was laid out against the burnt orange of the setting sun like a brand-new world. Mowgli had had no idea the Jungle was so big.

"Wow," Mowgli whispered. He had never seen anything like it in his life.

"Not bad, huh?" Baloo smiled. "So that's what you're leaving. And this . . ."

Baloo took Mowgli by his bony shoulders and turned him around, one mighty paw pushing back the leafy overgrowth to reveal another astonishing view.

"This is where you wanna go."

Mowgli stepped forward slowly, haltingly, as if under the spell of Kaa herself, mesmerized by the scene below. The slope of the mountain dropped to a green valley with pockets of yellow grain and brown grassland. In the center of the valley lay a group of wooden structures curved like the back of a pangolin, made of trees and rocks, their flanks lit by bursts of sun glowing from wooden sticks. They glowed. Mowgli stared breathlessly, then spoke in a low whisper.

"The Man-village . . ."

THE MAN-VILLAGE

THE MAN-CUB'S EYES refused to blink.

Mowgli stepped forward until his toes felt the rush of wind climbing up past the cliff's edge. He wanted to move closer to the alien landscape below, but that was as far as his feet could take him.

"It's so bright. Like the night stars fell to Earth," Mowgli said, trying to make sense of what he was seeing. It was beautiful. Even brighter than what the snake had shown him.

"Yup. You can always tell a Man-village by the Red Flower," Baloo said with a sigh. "They do love their Red Flower."

The man-cub watched as columns of smoke rose from the village like tall thin clouds, always tethered to the Red Flower but trying desperately to escape.

"The Red Flower doesn't seem so bad," Mowgli thought aloud.

"Not from here it doesn't," Baloo admitted. "But let it loose and it destroys everything it touches. Hard to imagine something so small and beautiful could be capable of such a thing."

Baloo looked at the man-cub for a long moment, then dropped down on all fours to Mowgli's level, his dark black eyes inches from the boy's wide brown ones. He was suddenly, unexpectedly, very serious.

"Stay away from that. You hear me? You should never play with it or bring it into the Jungle. You got that?"

"Why?" Mowgli asked.

"You got that?" Baloo growled. It was a command, not a question.

"Yeah, I got it."

"Good," Baloo said, satisfied that he had made his point. He finally dropped onto his backside to take a load off. But Mowgli didn't join him. The boy's attention had been pulled uncontrollably back to the glowing lights of the small Indian village.

"Baloo," he said quietly, "do you think that's where I'm from?"

"I don't know, kid. Could be. Does it look familiar?"

"I don't know. I don't remember it." Mowgli frowned, looking up into the star-filled darkness that hung above him. "All I remember is living with the wolves. My first memories are fighting with my brothers and sisters to get my share of whatever Akela had killed for us. The wolves were always my family. I don't know man."

And Mowgli wasn't sure he wanted to.

"What if they don't want me?" Mowgli continued after turning back to the Man-village. His face was lined with worry. "Then I won't have a people at all."

"Are you kidding me? A kid like you? Of course they're gonna want you," Baloo said, clapping Mowgli on the back and nearly sending him over the edge of the cliff. "The question is, do you want them?"

"I don't know," the boy said honestly. How could he know how he felt about creatures he had never met? He still didn't know where he truly belonged. "But Bagheera said I need a people."

"Bagheera," Baloo snorted. "There you go again,

listening to Bagheera. I'll tell you what. Why don't you stick around for a little while, just till winter, and help me out? Then *you* can decide. 'Cause I gotta tell you, kid, we make a pretty good team."

"Really?" Mowgli asked, his mood lifting for the first time since they'd reached the mountaintop.

"Really," Baloo assured him. "Your brains and my stomach, there's no stoppin' us. And if you decide you wanna leave, you leave. No rules. No *Bagheera*. Whattaya say?"

Mowgli couldn't see any reason to refuse.

"Okay," Mowgli said, grinning.

"Great!" Baloo grinned back. "That's just great, kid. Trust me, we're gonna have some real fun together."

Suddenly, the treetops all around them erupted with piercing squeaking sounds that reverberated off the mountain walls.

"Oh! Hear that?" Baloo grinned wider. "Right on time. The fun's about to start. Watch this, little brother. It's gonna blow your mind."

Half running, half sliding down the mountain trail, Baloo led a perplexed Mowgli to a better vantage point, looking out at a giant fig tree. The leaves swayed and danced in the wind.

"It's a tree," Mowgli said, unimpressed.

"But what's *on* the tree?" Baloo chuckled.

"Leaves?" Mowgli yawned.

"Those aren't leaves," Baloo sang.

All at once, the tree erupted, a torrent of black shapes exploding outward like the jetting spray from an elephant's trunk. They were bats, hundreds upon hundreds of them, their leathery wings beating at the night and blocking out the light of the stars. The high-pitched keening of the creatures, joined in unison, bounced off every surface at once, both a homing beacon and a peculiar kind of night music.

"See?" Baloo shrugged. "Every tribe has a song."

"Wow," was all Mowgli could say.

"C'mon," the old bear said as he put a hairy arm around his companion. "Who needs a Man-village when you got this, huh?"

Yeah, who needs it? thought Mowgli.

As they set off down the mountain path together, Mowgli couldn't help smiling.

ENEMY
AMONG US

THE DAY WRAPPED *the Jungle in its bright yellow arms.*

Sunlight filtered through the canopy, and pillars of light as tall and strong as elephants were warming the leaves on the ground where Mowgli wrestled with his siblings. Raksha looked at her brood with tenderness. They were so young. So small. So innocent.

But before she knew it, Mowgli was gone. He was running away from the others and back into the mouth of the cave. But this mouth had teeth—rows upon rows of razor-sharp teeth—and it rumbled like the purr of a cat.

Almost in slow motion, the cave mouth began to close around her man-cub. Raksha tried to run, tried to reach her baby, tried to stop the inevitable. . . .

Ami. Ami. Ami.

Raksha woke with a start. It was late in the evening and she had fallen asleep in her cave, but Gray was pawing at her nervously and calling to her.

"*Ami*, wake up."

Raksha shot up, eyes instinctively scanning the cave for her cubs. They were gone.

She burst out of the den and found she was the only wolf outside. Where were her brothers and sisters? Where was the rest of the pack?

Then she saw them, or she saw their eyes at least—peering fearfully out of their caves. They were trembling, afraid to come out. But why?

She slowly approached Council Rock, worried about what she might see but needing to see it nonetheless, needing to find her cubs.

And there, where Akela should have been, where their leader had once sat, was the loathsome figure of Shere Khan. He was spread out languorously, as if he truly belonged there, as if the throne were already his. Raksha's heart caught in her throat, but it was not the sight of the tiger that affected her as much as seeing her litter of cubs crawling all over him. They rolled off his back. They pawed at his whiskers. One pounced repeatedly at his casually undulating tail. They were in their enemy's grasp . . . and enjoying it.

Horrified, Raksha slowly, carefully moved closer. The screeching cry of a vulture protecting its prey called her attention to the rotting carcass of a young buck lying nearby. More cackling screams drew her eyes up to the trees, where dozens of the hideous scavengers, harbingers of doom, waited impatiently for Shere Khan to make his next kill.

Raksha stopped a good ten paces from the tiger, afraid to move any closer. Gray cowered behind her, his head poking out from under her belly, his tiny tail tucked up tight between his legs.

"Pups," she called. "It is time to go." But the little ones were caught up in their play and didn't heed their mother.

"Oh, did we wake you?" Shere Khan drawled. "My apologies."

"Finish the story, Shere Khan!" cried one of the cubs.

"Of course. The children do love their stories. Now, let's see," the mighty cat said, pausing to pick a morsel of buck meat from between his teeth with a finely sharpened claw. "Where was I?"

"The cuckoo bird!" another shouted.

"Ah, yes," Shere Khan said. "The cuckoo bird is too clever to waste time raising its young. Instead, it sneaks its eggs into the nests of simpler, less sensible birds. So when they hatch, the mothers mistake them for their own."

He paused his story as one of the larger pups playfully batted his paw at Shere Khan's tongue, reaching into the tiger's open mouth. Raksha instinctively held her breath until the cub moved on.

"And do you know what happens to their own chicks?" Shere Khan asked the group.

"What?" the pups all cried as one.

"They starve and die from neglect," Shere Khan said simply. Then he turned, directing his gaze at Raksha. "All because a mother loved a chick that wasn't her own."

Raksha smarted. His threat was clear, but she refused to show fear. Her eyes narrowed to angry slits.

"Time for sleep," she called to her young. "Come on, now."

Shere Khan stared into her eyes for a long moment, then, almost as an afterthought, motioned for the cubs to move along. Bouncing like newborns, they scampered back to their cave, Gray hurrying after them.

"They're so adorable." Shere Khan smiled. "I could just eat them up."

Raksha stood her ground, refusing to avert her eyes as she demanded, "Why are you doing this?"

"You know why," he said simply, running his tongue across the white tuft of hair on his chin to remove the last taste of buck blood.

"He's gone," Raksha assured the tiger. "That's what you wanted."

"Is that what I wanted?" Shere Khan rose to his feet. "He won't be gone forever. Mark my words. Sooner or later, they all come back, and they all become the same thing," he explained, his words hanging in the air like poison. He walked away, knowing full well that every eye in the wolf pack was on him.

"And by then you'll be begging me to save you."

MIDAIR
MANEUVERS

THE BEE SAW something strange in front of its home.

It was a floating beast that moved like an animal but had the appearance of a tree. It moved along a vine like a monkey but clawed at their honey like the mighty bear. It held a sharpened branch as long as the snake and as sharp as a panther claw. It was unlike any animal the bee had ever seen.

Mowgli hung from a harness he had designed himself, suspended on a lengthy rope he had woven from the plentiful vines in the area. As the bees investigated his presence, they were thwarted by the hide of protective leaves covering his body; this time, he had fashioned a barrier between his skin and the bees' stingers. He thrust his spear forward, breaking off a large piece of honeycomb. Before it could fall to the ground far below, he speared it and slipped it into a woven pouch slung across his back.

This could actually work, Mowgli thought, allowing himself a small smile as he balanced on the end of a rope that passed through a pulley at the cliff top and then dropped to the Jungle floor below.

"Tell him to go down to the second mark," Mowgli called to the giant squirrel, who had been enlisted to help with the honey retrieval process.

"Okay, it's your funeral," the squirrel chirped. He skittered down the rope toward the tree where Baloo lay lounging in the shade, enjoying a plethora of berries laid out across his ample belly. Around his midsection was the other end of the crudely fashioned rope, using Baloo's considerable weight as an anchor to balance Mowgli on the other end.

Beside Baloo three curious parties watched the proceedings.

"He looks like a four-legged banyan tree," noted the pangolin as he licked a few stray ants from his claw.

"Why does he *wear* leaves when he could *eat* leaves?" the pygmy hog asked, confused. The hornbill honked in agreement. It was all very perplexing.

"Hey, Baloo," the squirrel called. "Second mark."

"Ooh, ooh, watch this," the pangolin called to the others. "The tiny squirrel barks and the mighty bear moves."

With a sigh of discontent, Baloo made what he felt was a considerable effort to rise to his feet, spilling most of his afternoon snack.

"See? I told you," the pangolin chittered. "I told you!"

With surprising speed, Baloo whirled around, baring his claws and teeth at the unwelcome spectators, a thunderous roar climbing out of his throat to blow back their fur and feathers.

Instantly, they were gone, the hornbill taking flight, the pygmy hog darting into the undergrowth, and the pangolin rolling into a ball, praying that his thick scales would protect him. Even the giant squirrel flattened his body against the nearest tree, frozen in self-preservation mode.

Baloo harrumphed. "Yeah, that's what I thought." He lumbered closer to the cliff, the rope around his midsection remaining taut as Mowgli's weight pulled it forward. Baloo sauntered past several clearly defined lines drawn in the dirt, with little regard for how far he had gone.

High above, Mowgli was lowered slowly down the cliff side to the next patch of honeycombs, only to drop right past it. The boy reached out, but soon he was too low even to touch the target with his spear.

"Whoa, whoa, whoa!" Mowgli yelled down. "No, Baloo. I said the *second* mark!"

"What's he saying?" Baloo asked.

"The second mark!" Mowgli yelled.

"I can't hear him," Baloo said, turning to the giant squirrel. "Tell him I can't hear him."

The squirrel hustled back up the fifty feet of vine to Mowgli.

"Hey, Man-cub. He can't hear you."

"I know he can't hear me," Mowgli huffed, exasperated. "That's what *you're* supposed to be for."

"Second mark!" Mowgli yelled down again.

"What?" Baloo asked.

"Second mark!" Mowgli screamed.

Reluctantly, Baloo hefted his furry behind off the Jungle floor once again, searching the dirt for whatever Mowgli meant by the "second mark" and wondering exactly when he had signed on for all this physical exertion.

Silently returning to the scene with the utmost

caution, the hornbill, hog, and pangolin whispered among themselves.

"See?" the pangolin repeated. "He speaks and the bear obeys."

"Maybe the bear feels bad for him, y'know, 'cause . . ." The pygmy hog's voice trailed off.

"Because he knows the boy is sure to fall and die before the sun sets?" the pangolin asked.

"Yeah, that," the hog grunted.

"Yes, that's probably it," the pangolin agreed.

Far above them, Mowgli rose back up until he was directly across from the massive honeycomb . . . and stopped. He rolled his eyes. *Finally!*

"There you go, kid," Baloo called up. "That's the one!" The bear inhaled deeply, his keen sense of smell alerting his stomach to the impending feast.

Mowgli gouged his spear into the thick yellow surface, splitting off a chunk as large as his head. He wrestled it into his pouch and raised the spear again.

"Perfect," Baloo said, grinning. "Perfect. You set your mind to it, you can do anything. I told you you had potential."

Baloo licked his lips. "Look at all that potential."

After a few moments and multiple unnecessary observations by the scavengers, Baloo trotted eagerly

toward the cliff face, the taut rope lowering Mowgli
all the way to the Jungle floor.

"C'mere, you." Baloo grinned, his arms spread
wide in greeting. "You beautiful thing." Reaching
up, his huge padded paws moved right past Mowgli
to the honey-filled bag on his back. Baloo was
transfixed by the golden treasure, a glint in his eye.
He seemed unable to restrain himself, as though he'd
gone mad with hunger.

"Hey," Mowgli snapped as he struggled to pull
himself out of the harness without Baloo's help.
"What kind of crazy animal talks to his food? Are
you getting the *dewanee*?"

"The only madness I've got is a madness for a
meal. Come to Papa, my little morsels." And with
that, Baloo walked away with the honeycombs,
forgetting that he was still connected to Mowgli.
Half out of his harness, the man-cub quickly rose
right back up the cliff side, dangling precariously.

"No, wait!" Mowgli cried, his limbs flailing
wildly. "No, Baloo. Waaaait!"

A short distance away, the giant squirrel joined
the other scavengers and made himself comfortable.
He commented to the others under his breath.

"Pull up a log, fellas. This is just getting good."

THE RIVER

THE LAZY RIVER sighed as it drifted around every bend and over every boulder.

Once Baloo and Mowgli had stowed his climbing gear and added a good portion of the honeycomb to Baloo's stash, the two had rewarded themselves with a late-night float.

With the man-cub lying on the downy pillow of the bear's stomach, Baloo drifted downstream on his back, munching contentedly on handfuls of his new snack. To the bear, relaxation was an art, and Baloo was a particularly gifted artist. They passed beneath the horizontal limbs of an ever-growing banyan tree, listening to the gentle lapping of the river kissing the shore. The night was warm, the water was cool, and the honey was delicious.

"This is the life, partner," Baloo said with a sigh.

"Yeah," Mowgli agreed, stretching and yawning. "This is the life."

"You got that right," Baloo said between mouthfuls. The moonlight glistened on the lazily undulating water, making it twinkle like the starry sky above.

Mowgli hadn't felt so at peace in a long, long time. Maybe ever. As he drifted past gentle waterfalls and under lush canopies, he couldn't help thinking that maybe, at last, he had found where he belonged. The muscles in his neck and back, once as taut as Kaa's coils, finally released their strangling hold, allowing him to truly let go and relax.

Beyond content, Baloo began to hum his familiar tune once again. But this time, Mowgli joined in.

"Forget about your worries and your strife," they sang in unison.

But a sudden rustling in the brush brought their duet to an abrupt end. Mowgli bolted upright.

"Baloo," he said, pointing. "Look."

Quickly, Baloo rolled over into a fighting stance, motioning for the man-cub to get behind him. Slowly, cautiously, they pushed through the drifting water to the muddy bank where the sound seemed to come from.

"Show yourself," Baloo growled, his laid-back attitude instantly pushed aside by an aggressive intensity.

The leaves rustled, then parted as Bagheera stepped forward. He was weak and tired and still smarting from recent wounds, but all Mowgli could see was his old friend and mentor.

"Bagheera!" he cried, splashing out of the water to throw his arms around the old cat's neck, burrowing his face into his thick black hide.

"Are you all right?" Bagheera asked. He pawed the man-cub, searching for scars or signs of a struggle.

"Yeah, yeah, I'm okay." Mowgli laughed, his unbridled energy causing him to dance from foot to foot. "I can't believe you found me. I was so worried about you."

"It was not easy," Bagheera said, the monumental journey finally catching up with him. He sank down by the water's edge and lapped wearily at the pool.

"Hey, I want you to meet my friend," Mowgli said. "This is Baloo."

Baloo slowly stepped out of the water.

"Hello, Bagheera."

"Oh, right! You two know each other!" Mowgli cried happily.

"I was so worried about you," Mowgli continued, his words tumbling out faster than figs from a shaken tree. "I didn't know what happened to you. I got lost and I was alone and then I met Baloo and he saved me from a big snake and now we're working together!"

"Really?" Bagheera said in mock wonder. "That's a new wrinkle. I was not aware that sloth bears worked."

"Oh, is that one of your Rules of the Jungle?" Baloo threw back. "Fascinating. No one can fill an afternoon like Bagheera talking about the rules."

Mowgli noticed something in their tones; the bear and the panther didn't seem to like each other very much.

"Thank you for watching him," allowed Bagheera. "Come, Man-cub. Let's be on our way."

"But, Bagheera, Baloo's my new pack now," pleaded Mowgli. "I wanna stay here."

"Yessiree," Baloo sang, lifting a giggling Mowgli up onto his shoulder. "And if I may say so, that's a real talented cub we've got here."

"You mean *man-cub*," Bagheera growled, his patience wearing thin.

"Yeah. Cub. Man-cub. Mowgli. Whatever he is, he's great."

"I take it you know where a man-cub belongs."

"The Man-village, right?" Mowgli interrupted. He wanted to cut off the old cat before he could get any further. "I thought that, too. But I can be a man here, right, Baloo? Here, take a look. Come check it out!"

Bagheera watched as Mowgli eagerly bolted back across the river, splashing loud enough for any predator within two hundred strides to hear him.

"Mowgli!" Bagheera called, but the boy had already disappeared through the brush on the opposite bank. The mighty cat sighed with fatigue. After so many moons of searching, Bagheera had finally found the man-cub, and he was already running off.

So once again, Bagheera ran after Mowgli.

THE **CONFRONTATION**

MOWGLI CHARGED across the Jungle,
weaving like a kite, hardly touching the ground
with his feet.

He knew he could convince Bagheera. He had to.
If he could just show him how far he'd come, all the
things he'd accomplished, Bagheera would have to
let him stay.

The silent cat followed close behind, up the
winding embankment toward Baloo's cave.

"Hey!" called the pygmy hog as Mowgli ran past.

"Hi, Man-cub!" The pangolin waved. He was
holding one end of a makeshift leash fashioned from
vines, with the pygmy hog at the other end. The
pygmy hog was happily being led through the forest
tethered to another scavenger. Clearly, Mowgli's

presence had made a profound impact in that part of the Jungle.

"Hey, guys," Mowgli called back without hesitating. The smaller animals' curious arrangement didn't seem out of place to the man-cub, but Bagheera was momentarily thrown off his stride, staring in wonderment at the bizarre relationship. What had the man-cub been up to while under that bear's influence?

"We going climbing later?" the pangolin called after Mowgli, but the boy was already out of earshot. The pangolin turned to the pygmy hog. "Because it's my turn to go up."

"Oh, no, you went up last time," the pygmy hog said. "It's my turn to fly."

"Oh, yeah, right. A flying pig. Dream on," the pangolin replied.

Bagheera caught up to Mowgli.

"Don't be mad, okay?" Mowgli asked.

"Why would I be mad?" Bagheera responded, already suspicious.

"'Cause you're always mad when I do stuff, but you gotta promise not to be mad this time. And then no breaking that promise, right?"

It was a promise the weary cat was unable to make.

"Show me," he said. "Then I will decide."

Unable to contain his enthusiasm, Mowgli scampered up to a small lean-to he had constructed outside Baloo's cave. It consisted of thick support branches and a roof of thatched twigs and leaves that protected the various tools he had made, all hanging neatly from hooks. He had labored over the structure and its contents for days upon days, and his pride was evident.

Bagheera hesitated. This did not belong in the Jungle. It looked more like one of man's traps than anything else. He was wary of getting too close, but Mowgli ran inside.

"These are vines I use on the cliff. I twirled them together to make them longer and stronger. See?" Mowgli tugged with all his might on the vine rope, but it wouldn't break.

"And this is the thing I use to hold myself up," he said, proudly displaying the harness he had fashioned. "It could probably even hold you if I adjusted it a little. You wanna try?"

"I think not," Bagheera snorted, but before he

could say anything further, the man-cub erupted again with excitement.

"Ohhh, and the pouch I made. It hangs over my shoulder when I go up to collect the—Oh! The really cool part is inside. Check it out!"

Mowgli darted out of the lean-to and into Baloo's cave, his eagerness radiating like the summer sun at midday. Bagheera eyed the entrance to the dark den with concern. It was not wise, even for one as strong as he, to venture blindly into an enclosed space, but slowly, cautiously, he followed the man-cub inside.

Bagheera's eyes quickly adjusted to the darkness, and what he saw made no sense.

"Lookit!" Mowgli said, throwing his arms wide as a proud grin spread across his face. "It's a honey stash! For winter. Baloo says I'm finally reaching my true potential. What do you think?"

Bagheera was speechless. The cave was stacked with pile after towering pile of honeycombs. Mounds as big as bison filled every corner, rising from the dusty floor to the damp ceiling. There was barely room to walk.

"Have you lost your mind?" Bagheera gasped.

"You said you wouldn't get mad," Mowgli protested.

"Did you listen to anything Akela taught you? There is no place in the Jungle for these tricks. You want to do this, you do this in a Man-village."

That wasn't what Mowgli wanted to hear. He wanted Bagheera to be proud of him. He looked up as Baloo entered the cave and squeezed between two gargantuan honeycomb stacks.

"But I'm helping Baloo," Mowgli explained. "To get ready for hibernation."

"Bears do not hibernate in a jungle!" Bagheera snapped at Baloo. "What are you teaching him?"

Mowgli's mouth hung open. Was that true? Had he been lied to all that time? He looked to Baloo, expecting him to set Bagheera straight, but the bear averted his eyes.

"Never hurts to be prepared." Baloo shrugged.

"Listen to me, you con artist," Bagheera began, laying into him. "He may not know your games, but I do. He's leaving now."

Mowgli ran to Bagheera, desperate. "No. I don't wanna go."

"You do not have a choice!" Bagheera growled.

"Now hold on," Baloo started. "You can't tell the boy what to do. . . ."

"I belong here," Mowgli protested. He was desperate. He had truly hoped that could be his home. "He's my pack now."

"He is using you," Bagheera spat.

"And *he's* controlling you," Baloo barked back.

Instantly, Bagheera crouched lower to the ground, ready to pounce, a deep growl rumbling past his glistening teeth.

"Whoa. Okay, okay," said Baloo, his hands raised as he attempted to pacify the warring parties in his home. "Let's all settle down the growling and teeth baring for a minute, okay? Everybody relax. No sense getting our fur all bunched up over this."

Bagheera glared at the big bear.

Mowgli scowled at Bagheera. He was no longer a cub. He didn't need the old cat or anyone else to make his decisions for him. He opened his mouth to say something, but it seemed Baloo and Bagheera were not finished.

"Besides," Baloo continued, "look outside. Sun's dropping off faster than a molting peacock feather. It's getting late. Too late to travel."

Bagheera looked outside.

"So why don't we all just settle down, take a load off, have a little honey. . . ."

"I do not eat honey," Bagheera snarled.

"Okay, to each his own," Baloo said, snapping off a generous chunk for himself. "For now, let's just get a good night's sleep. We can talk about all this in the morning, okay?"

Bagheera didn't like conceding to Baloo, even on such a small point, but there was no sense in arguing.

"Fine," he finally said. "But we are leaving at first light."

The panther slid out of the cave and into the night to find a tree to sleep in.

"Well, that went well," Baloo said to himself dryly. "It's a shame he doesn't come to visit more often."

Mowgli glanced at the bear, who had started to curl up in the cave, then looked out at the shadow of the retreating panther. The man-cub felt pulled in too many directions. He knew it was his own fault; he wanted Bagheera's approval but fought his advice, and he loved the life Baloo lived, but now he wasn't sure if that was the life he should be living. It all made the man-cub more tired than he'd been in his entire life.

A **NOISE** IN
THE **NIGHT**

THE JUNGLE WAS COLD.

An encroaching mist enveloped the Jungle tree by tree, wiping away details as the world faded to white. A bone-chilling wind from the north swept through the valleys and slipped through the cracks in the rocky outcroppings, seeking out the shivering animals trying to hide from its icy fingers. Mowgli had never, in all his years, felt such a chill in his bones, and it made his lean frame shake like the tail of a cobra. All he wanted to do was climb into his den and curl up next to Raksha with Gray and the other pups, to snuggle in where it was nice and warm and safe.

But when he reached the cave, it was empty. All the caves were empty. And fear ate at his belly like a worm.

"This is not your home," boomed a voice from the top of Council Rock. "You wear the skin of the wolf, but you are not wolf."

Mowgli looked down at himself and saw that he wore the hide of Akela over his head and shoulders like a cloak. Revolted, he yanked the fur from his body and threw it down. He tried to protest, but no sound escaped his lips.

Mowgli turned back to the cave, but it was no longer Raksha's cave; it was Baloo's. Mowgli ran inside, but it also was empty and barren.

"This is not your home," boomed the same powerful voice. "You do not belong here, Man-cub." Mowgli covered his ears, desperately trying to block out the voice as it stampeded around the inside of his head. He didn't want to hear it. He just wanted to go home.

"This is your home." The voice echoed and Mowgli looked up to see the scarred mask of Shere Khan looking down at him, a grin splitting his face in two. The tiger opened his jaws wide, wide enough for the man-cub to step inside, where the raging blossom of the Red Flower was waiting for him. Then the voice boomed again, laughing:

"Welcome home, Man-cub."

Mowgli broke out of his nightmare, arms flailing. It was the fifth or sixth time he had woken up that night. He couldn't seem to get comfortable. The

banyan tree leaves he had fashioned into a bed kept
poking at him. A mosquito had been feeding on him
on and off since Baloo had started his traditional
chuffing night noises. From outside the cave,
the sounds of the night that he usually found so
comforting kept rousing him just as he started to fall
asleep.

How had things gotten so complicated? This
wasn't a problem he could solve with one of his
tricks. All he wanted to do was find a home, but
there was nowhere he fit in. The wolf pack was
no longer safe. The Man-village was strange and
unfamiliar. Staying with Baloo had felt right, and
Baloo was all for it, but now Bagheera said this was
not his place, either. Who was right? Bagheera?
Baloo? Neither of them? He felt more than
confused. The pounding in his head was like a river
raging between his ears.

A blinding ray of dazzling orange light broke
through the cracks in the thick Jungle canopy and
into the cave. The sun was just cresting the tree line,
shining directly into Mowgli's eyes. There would be
no more sleeping for him.

Mowgli sat up. Beyond the sounds of the night
birds, the irritating whine of the mosquitoes, and the

gruff, rumbling snores of Baloo was a sound Mowgli did not recognize. A high-pitched blast of . . . of what?

Mowgli stood, curious, and slipped silently past the slumbering mass of matted hair that was Baloo and out of the cave. The man-cub stepped cautiously across the ground as Bagheera had taught him, holding his breath and avoiding sticks and leaves that would give away his location to the panther himself in the tree above.

Again he heard the high, keening wail of what sounded like an animal in trouble. A warning or an alarm of some kind. Mowgli moved quickly but quietly toward the distant sound.

Fresh dew, winking with reflected sunlight, dripped from the leaves and vines as Mowgli pushed his way through the foliage and up onto a gently sloping hill that would give him a view of the grass valley. The sounds seemed to be coming from there. At the crest of the hill, Mowgli craned his neck to see what was happening below. He froze, startled. He didn't know what he had expected, but it wasn't that.

A herd of elephants, agitated and trumpeting in shrill blasts, moved anxiously around a mud pit. They approached, then retreated in darting movements. To Mowgli, it looked like those mighty, unstoppable creatures were *frightened*.

But what could frighten an entire herd of the largest animals in the Jungle? he wondered.

He had to find out.

THE GREAT
ELEPHANTS

MOWGLI KNEW the old cat wouldn't approve, but he couldn't stop himself.

He slid silently down the embankment to the valley below and sprinted across the grassy plain to see what was wrong. He had never been so close to the elephant pack before and they towered over him like mighty gray mountains. Suddenly aware of his presence, the huge pachyderms reared back, disturbed by the intruder. Whatever the problem was, a young man-cub racing among their stomping feet was not helping.

Mowgli barely had time to notice that before an intense blow to the side of his head sent him reeling. As quickly as he could recover, he rose and turned, but before the man-cub could get his bearings, a second elephant's trunk, thick as a small tree, swatted him away, that one slamming into his side and nearly crushing a rib. Suddenly, Mowgli realized just how dangerous a situation he had put himself in. He was like a mosquito to the gargantuan creatures and they could crush him with one step.

Mowgli moved back and quickly dropped to his knees. As Bagheera had taught him, he bowed, offering respect, hoping it wasn't too late.

The bull elephant nearest to the man-cub paused, his mighty trunk raised to issue another, perhaps fatal, blow. He looked down, curious, at the tiny brown creature in the respectful pose. If the human was not there to attack them, then why was he there?

The elephants, still agitated, turned away from Mowgli and back to the mud pit. Slowly, gently, he rose to his feet and moved carefully through the walls of weathered gray hide to the edge of the pit. His heart fluttered like a baby bird in his chest when he saw what had taken the entire herd to the brink of panic.

And he believed he could help.

Mowgli flew, as fast as his feet could carry him, to his lean-to. He snatched up his tools and hurried back the way he had come.

Bagheera lifted his head from the branch where he had been sleeping. Was that Mowgli he had heard? What was that boy up to now?

Bagheera dropped to the ground, the thick pads of his paws absorbing the impact, then slunk into Baloo's cave.

Mowgli was nowhere to be seen. There was only the bear and the echo of his rumbling snores.

"Wake up, you lazy good-for-nothing," Bagheera said, shaking the big brown lump a bit more violently than absolutely necessary.

"What? What?" Baloo said, scratching himself lazily. "Oh, it's you. I had kinda hoped you were just a bad dream." He rolled over to go back to sleep.

"The man-cub is gone," Bagheera informed him. "I thought you might know where he was going."

"I'm sure he'll be back soon," Baloo said, rubbing the sleep out of his eyes. "Whatever he's doing, I trust him. He's a smart kid. He's smarter than I am."

"You can say that again," Bagheera sighed.

"Don't underestimate him."

Bagheera ignored the bear.

"I am going after him."

"All right. Fine. I'm up, I'm up. And I'm coming, too," Baloo said, shaking his head to clear it and standing as quickly as his considerable bulk would allow.

"You will only slow me down."

"Not on your life," Baloo countered.

"Do not make promises you clearly cannot keep," Bagheera snorted, turning to leave. "We both know how that turns out."

"One time!" Baloo bellowed. "One time over fifteen seasons ago, but you refuse to let it die!"

"Because I almost *did* die," Bagheera snarled back. "Thanks to you. Or rather, no thanks to you. An animal's word is his bond in the Jungle and yours is worthless."

With that, Bagheera left the cave, quickly moving to pick up Mowgli's trail while it was still fresh. Baloo sighed heavily.

"What kind of creature wakes someone from a perfectly good sleep to yell at him?" Baloo yawned. "A bear can't even take a nap in his own cave anymore, I tell you."

Across the Jungle, Mowgli was already sidestepping down the steep hillside to the elephants' grassy field, reconfiguring his tools as he ran.

Moments later, Bagheera broke through the tree line at the top of the hill, his keen eyes searching the countryside for his charge. There. In the valley. The man-cub. Surrounded by an entire pack of elephants.

"Man-cub!" Bagheera cried, but the boy was too far away and too involved in what he was doing to hear. Before Bagheera could cry out again, Mowgli disappeared from sight. Where had he gone? Behind one of the great elephants . . . or trampled beneath one?

"Where is he?" Baloo gasped as he finally caught up, huffing and puffing from the run up the hill. He grabbed hold of a tree trunk and bent over, trying to catch his breath.

"There," Bagheera spat. "Is that your teaching?"

Baloo lifted his head to follow Bagheera's cold gaze.

"Whoa!" Baloo huffed. "I never taught him to mess with elephants. I'm lazy, not suicidal."

"Let's go," Bagheera said, racing toward the man-cub. "Before it's too late!"

MAN-CUB
TRIUMPHANT

MOWGLI BELIEVED he could do this.

He clambered out of the mud pit, carrying the ends of several vines in his teeth. He knew that one wrong step could mean death at the end of a dozen massive ivory tusks, but he approached the largest bull elephant and held out the vine anyway. The pack leader still didn't understand what the tiny hairless monkey wanted. Frustrated but unwilling to give up, Mowgli moved on to the largest female of the pack, the matriarch, again holding out the vine, tugging on it a few times to show her what to do. The elephant was unsure how that would help, but she took the vine with her trunk and pulled.

Mowgli urged her back, away from the pit. He slapped at the thick, impenetrable hide of her legs as hard as he could, knowing that it would have all the impact of a butterfly's wing on his own skin. But she got the message. Slowly, carefully, she began to back up.

Whether they understood or were simply copying her movements, several other elephants took hold of the vines with their massive trunks and began to move backward, away from the pit. The vines grew taut and slowly, inch by inch, rose from the pit like snakes from a viper den.

Mowgli raced to the edge to look down into the darkness, where a keening *elephant calf* was rising out of the pit. It was working! Mowgli's heart sang.

Bagheera and Baloo stopped at the bottom of the hill as they saw what the boy had done. The baby clambered out of the pit, alive and unharmed, thanks to the ropes and slings Mowgli had fashioned.

"Well, would ya look at that?" Baloo shook his head in amazement. "Our boy is all grown up. Come to think of it, maybe it *was* me that told him to mess with elephants."

Mowgli worked to remove his modified harness from the elephant calf, unwinding more vines from its stocky gray legs. The calf was nearly as tall as the man-cub but a tiny baby compared to the rest of his tribe. Mowgli spoke soothingly to the little one the whole time, not knowing if the calf could understand the words.

"It's okay, little guy. You're okay. And your *ami*'s here and your father's here. The whole pack was worried about you, but you're okay, and they're gonna take you home now."

The elephant calf looked into the man-cub's eyes. He knew that this strange creature had helped him out of a dark, scary place and had brought him back to his family.

Mowgli stepped back and the calf galloped quickly to his mother, nuzzling his muddy head against her rough skin. Mowgli felt warmth in his chest spread quickly to his face, a pride that brushed over him like a sudden wind.

The pack walked slowly away, finally calm now that they were reunited, but not before the calf's mother paused to look back at the man-cub—a long silent look that could only be one of gratitude.

Stunned and impressed, Baloo and Bagheera stared at the receding pack of elephants as Mowgli walked past them.

"Hey, guys," he said, climbing the hill toward Baloo's cave. Bagheera and Baloo looked at each other.

"You gotta admit, he's special," Baloo said with a grin.

"I know the boy is special," Bagheera said quietly. "I found him. I raised him. But he is in danger."

"Yeah," Baloo said, serious for the first time. "He told me. He's being hunted by a tiger."

"Not just any tiger. Shere Khan."

"Shere Khan's hunting him?" Baloo said breathlessly.

"Yes."

"Wow," Baloo said.

He watched the shrinking silhouette of Mowgli disappear over the top of the hill, into the rising sun.

"But you know him. If you send that boy to the Man-village, they'll ruin him."

Bagheera didn't respond.

"We should send him back to the wolf pack," Baloo suggested. "Who's their alpha? Akela, he can protect him."

"Akela is dead," Bagheera said sadly.

"What?"

"Shere Khan killed him. And he will stop at nothing until he has this boy. Nothing. The only way we save him is if he goes to that Man-village."

Baloo had no response, staring up at the spot where Mowgli once had been.

Bagheera lowered his head. He was desperate. And Baloo could see it in his dark face and tired eyes.

"Please, Baloo. You're the only one he'll listen to."

BETRAYED

FOR THE FIRST TIME in his entire life, Baloo was at a loss for words.

Outside the cave, Mowgli placed his tools back on their hooks and began to adjust his harness as Baloo shuffled up hesitantly.

"Hey—hey kid," Baloo said, stammering.

"Hey, Baloo?" Mowgli started quietly. "That pit. The one the elephant calf fell in. Was that a man trap? Did men make that on purpose?"

Mowgli couldn't fathom why anyone, man or beast, would make something so awful. So cruel.

"I don't know, kid. Maybe. Probably. They've done it before."

"That's what I thought," Mowgli said, an anger in his voice that Baloo hadn't heard before. "Then I want nothing to do with man."

Baloo was silent for a moment. He didn't know how to respond to that. Especially because of what he was about to do.

"So, hey, that was pretty cool," he finally said. "What you did back there."

"Bagheera didn't think so," Mowgli said tersely.

"No, I talked to him. He was impressed."

"He was?" Mowgli asked quickly. He could barely hide his excitement as he looked in the bear's eyes to see if he spoke the truth.

"Oh, yeah. I mean, the elephants, they don't talk to anyone. That was—wow."

Mowgli grinned as he finished up with the harness and tossed it back on its hook. Baloo said he had impressed Bagheera. *Wow.*

"And listen," Baloo continued awkwardly, "I know this maybe isn't what you really wanna hear . . . but I think Bagheera's right."

"What do you mean?" Mowgli asked. "Right about what?"

"Well, let's face it," Baloo said, turning away so he wouldn't have to look at the boy. "You don't belong here."

His words hit Mowgli like a paw across the face.

"You're a man. Right? And—and you're

growing up. Who knows? You might like it in that Man-village."

"Wait, what are you talking about? We're partners."

"I know, kid. I know. But the truth is you just don't fit in here."

Mowgli felt like the ground he stood on had suddenly collapsed beneath him, his insides swirling as if he were falling.

"This is no home for a man," Baloo continued. "It's not your place. The Man-village is where you belong. See?"

Mowgli stared at the bear in disbelief. *What happened to being a team? What happened to staying together?* The man-cub felt like he was being attacked from all sides. He could take only so many jabs and pokes before he crumbled and fell like a honeycomb.

And suddenly, Mowgli realized what had happened. He felt the pressure of welling tears behind his eyes.

"Bagheera made you say it, didn't he? Didn't he?"

"Kid," was all Baloo could say.

Mowgli's mind was spinning. How had Baloo turned against him so quickly? He was the one who had said that Mowgli could be who he wanted to be.

That it was his song to sing. That it was up to him. But Baloo had lied. He was just as bad as the rest of them.

Mowgli's heart broke, cutting his words into pieces.

"Just—stay away from me. I thought you were my friend."

Baloo turned to reach for the man-cub, but it was too late.

Unable to stop the tears from falling, Mowgli ran from his lean-to into the thick of the Jungle, away from his home, away from his friend, away from everything.

INTO THE
TIGER'S DEN

A TWITCHY JACKAL darted nervously down the path.

He was in a hurry but not at all eager to get where he was going. One rarely looked forward to an audience with Shere Khan.

But the jackal had information he knew Shere Khan was looking for. Information that might prove quite valuable. Information about the man-cub.

Word traveled fast in the Jungle, and the jackal knew he must be fleet of foot if he was to reach Shere Khan with the news first. And he must be first if he wanted to receive any reward.

Perhaps the leftovers of a recently felled bison would be his. Or he might be given the bones of a wild pig, not yet picked clean by the powerful tiger. He had even heard that Shere Khan sometimes visited the Man-village to kill cattle. Certainly, even an animal as big and powerful as Shere Khan couldn't devour an entire cow before it went bad. And whatever was left could be bestowed on helpful, informative jackal.

The jackal left the well-worn path and cut through the underbrush to a hidden clearing he normally stayed far away from. Every animal in the Jungle knew the location of Shere Khan's lair. And few were foolish enough to venture there purposely.

"Excuse me, oh great Shere Khan," the jackal said meekly, bowing his head and averting his eyes as he entered the clearing.

"A visitor?" Shere Khan asked, mild amusement in his voice as he looked up from the latest in a long string of midday naps. "I so rarely get visitors these days."

"I'm sorry to intrude, Mighty One," the jackal continued, "but I have news that you will want to hear."

"News? What news could a mangy scavenger such as you have that would be of interest to me? Perhaps if you stepped closer I might find a better use for you." Shere Khan licked his lips and the jackal felt a shudder run down his spine like a trickle of cold river water.

"It's about the man-cub," the jackal spat out before Shere Khan could do something rash.

The tiger stood. The jackal had his full attention.

"Speak," Shere Khan said sternly. "If you have information, out with it."

"He—he is here," the jackal stuttered, his eyes glued firmly to the ground. He could not bear to look into the tiger's sparkling amber eyes.

"*Here?*" Shere Khan roared.

"Not here exactly," the jackal corrected himself, "but still in the Jungle. He has not joined a Man-village. He was seen several days' walk from here. He was seen with an elephant pack."

"With elephants?" Shere Khan mused. "How unusual."

"And useful?" the jackal asked hopefully.

"Ahhh." Shere Khan nodded, moving slowly toward his visitor. "You hoped to trade this rumor for something to fill your belly, is that it?"

"Yes, Your Greatness." The jackal bowed. "If it pleases you, most powerful Shere Khan."

"Well, if pleasing me is what you seek," the tiger

said with a smile, "then I can assure you that you won't be disappointed."

The tiger leapt at the jackal, and in a flash of blood and terror, Shere Khan was very pleased. For all tigers with full mouths and full bellies are happy tigers, indeed.

THE **MONKEY**

MOWGLI WAS ALONE in the Jungle.

He sat, legs swinging free, high in the wide
spreading branches of a peepal tree, where no
panther or bear would find him. He picked at the
light gray bark absentmindedly, his feet dangling in
open air. His head was too full of other thoughts to
do much else.

It seemed that everywhere he went, someone was
trying to tell him what to do and where to go. No
one seemed to want him—no one but the tiger, and
he just wanted to fill his belly.

Mowgli felt angry and betrayed and lonely all
at the same time, like a bird pushed out of the nest
and told never to come back. Maybe he didn't truly
belong anywhere. Not with the wolves. Not with
Baloo. Certainly not with man. If no one wanted

him, if he was just a thorn in everyone's paw, maybe he *was* better off alone.

He picked a fig off the tree and threw it angrily at the tree trunk. It hit with a hollow *thunk* . . . followed immediately by a second *thunk*. That was odd.

Mowgli picked a second fig, threw it, and once again heard the sound of two figs hitting the trunk. He looked around, and on a branch above and behind him was a monkey. The monkey seemed friendly, and truthfully, Mowgli was just happy to have the company.

"Oh, hey," Mowgli said. The man-cub turned back to his figs and threw another one. But this time he saw a second fig join his in its path to the trunk. Mowgli twirled around and saw the monkey pick up another fig, hopping lightly from foot to foot, eager to throw again. The little guy was copying him.

Mowgli threw another fig and the monkey did the same. Mowgli tossed a fig into the air and so did the monkey. Mowgli flopped over the edge of the tree limb, hanging by his legs. The monkey followed suit.

"You're funny, you know that?" Mowgli said, unable to suppress the hint of a smile breaking through his dark mood. As if sensing the man-cub's mood change, the monkey edged closer, dropping down to sit on Mowgli's branch only a few paces away.

Mowgli put his hands on his head and the monkey imitated the action, looking silly. Mowgli laughed. He stood on one leg and so did the monkey. It was so curious, so interesting, that Mowgli took no notice of the dozens of other creatures slowly closing in behind him.

Without warning, two hairy muscular arms dropped from the branches above him and scooped the man-cub up under his arms.

"Whoa! Hey!" Mowgli cried as he felt himself flying through the air with dozens of leering monkeys. One after the next lifted him, and passed him on. This was no game. The monkeys were stealing the man-cub.

Rising higher and higher through the dense foliage, Mowgli had never felt so vulnerable, so out of control. He flailed, trying to grab on to something, anything, but his hands grasped only air.

Above the treetops, higher than the teak or nimba or banyan grew, Mowgli was hurled into open air.

The world spun around him. The trees were up

and the clouds were down. Then he was caught, and the whole process began again.

The monkeys were moving faster and Mowgli was growing truly scared. He was out of control and at the mercy of hundreds of screeching hairy creatures. His life was literally in their hands.

The panther was desperate.

Baloo and Bagheera had been tracking Mowgli ever since he had darted out of the cave, but they had never imagined anything like this. Looking up with alarm, they saw the trees filled with screeching monkeys and then glimpsed the man-cub's small brown body plummeting from high above.

"Mowgli!" Bagheera cried, fearing he would see the boy killed before his very eyes. But far above, another monkey snatched the man-cub out of the air, lifting him higher before flipping him to the next set of hands.

"Mowgli, hold on!" Baloo yelled. "We're coming!"

Instantly, the sky was filled with projectiles as the simian horde pelted Bagheera and Baloo with rocks

and twigs, hurling anything that might slow the
two down. The fierce black cat darted and dodged
to avoid the missiles, but Baloo caught a sharp stone
right to the nose.

"You blasted tree-dwelling bug eaters!" he
yelled.

They quickly lost sight of Mowgli in the upper
canopy. But they didn't stop running. "There!"
Bagheera cried as Mowgli's body dropped through
the canopy and into view once again. He put on
an extra burst of speed, leaving Baloo behind but
narrowing the gap between himself and Mowgli. He
had to reach the man-cub before they disappeared
from his view.

Suddenly, Bagheera saw they were nearing the
edge of the tree line, approaching a sheer drop into
a deep ravine only a few strides away. It was now or
never. The panther leapt into the air.

For a moment, it was as if time stopped:
Bagheera, in midair, reaching desperately for the
man-cub; Mowgli spinning through the trees, mere
feet, perhaps even inches, away, reaching back. The
black fur of the panther's paws brushed the tips of
the man-cub's dirty brown fingers . . . but could not
take hold.

"Bagheera!" Mowgli cried, falling away from his protector as he was dragged down into the ravine by the army of screeching primates.

Bagheera landed in a pile, all legs and whipping tail, cursing himself as he attempted to catch his breath and watched his charge disappear in the foliage below. A moment later, Baloo appeared, huffing and puffing and visibly upset.

"Mowgli!" he cried. "Mowgliiii!" But the boy was gone.

"What was that?" Baloo wheezed, turning to Bagheera. "Why do they want the man-cub? Where are they taking him?"

"I think I might know," Bagheera said, "but it is far from here and I cannot let you slow me down." He started to walk away.

"Wait," Baloo said. "All those monkeys, you're gonna need help."

"I am loathe to admit it, but you may be right," Bagheera said impatiently. "But not from someone I cannot count on—who will disappear to eat or sleep or whatever else strikes his fancy when I need him the most. No, thank you. I am better off alone."

"We were cubs!" Baloo yelled. "I was hungry. How was I to know you'd go and fall in the river?"

"Because you were supposed to be holding me! That was our agreement. I nearly drowned because you wanted a papaya!"

"Correction: a lot of papayas."

"This is pointless," Bagheera chuffed. "I'm leaving."

"Now you listen to me," Baloo said, moving right up into Bagheera's face, snout to muzzle. It was a foolish thing for anyone to do, getting that close to an angry panther, but particularly foolish for someone whom the panther already disliked. Bagheera looked ready to take out his frustrations on the bear once and for all.

"I can't change the past," Baloo continued. "And I'm sorry for what I did. But if that boy is in danger, and I sure do think he is, then he's gonna need both of us and there's nothing you can say or do that's gonna stop me."

The two powerful creatures stared each other down for a moment longer, until, finally, Bagheera relented.

"Time we spend fighting is time we could be helping Mowgli," the panther said. "If you mean what you say, then we must move. Even at full speed, I fear in my bones that we may be too late."

THE **LOST CITY**

THE MAN-CUB flew through the air.

Mowgli, as he was passed from one large monkey to another, as often upside down as right side up, quickly lost track of where he was or how far they had traveled. From hand to hand, from vine to vine, up the scowling face of a cliff, the primates carried their unwilling victim over miles of rugged landscape until they reached the land of the Bandar-log.

Mowgli truly feared no one in the Jungle— well, almost no one—a fact that Bagheera would assert was his fatal flaw. But even the man-cub felt a strange sickening feeling in his stomach surrounded by so many agitated creatures. He hoped they couldn't smell the fear on him, but there was no way he could hide it from himself. He was scared.

Finally, after what seemed like an eternity, he once again felt his feet on solid ground.

Mowgli turned to survey the area where he'd been dropped and froze in place as his eyes fell on the bizarre landscape. A mammoth structure rose before him, unlike anything he had ever seen in the Jungle. The graceful curves of the banyan trees and lush colors of the ivy were gone, replaced by the straight lines and right angles of something built of rock, and Mowgli was standing at its doorway.

It towered over him like a great stone mountain, steps and plateaus and arches all carved from its belly to allow passage through it. It was hard and cold and rigid, blotting out the sun like a mighty hill seen from the valley below. This place was an invader in the Jungle.

The langur monkeys urged the man-cub forward and he reluctantly stepped through the ancient stone arch, overgrown with moss and vines, and into the gaping darkness beyond.

The forest of stone closed in around the man-cub.

Mowgli moved slowly through shafts of light and shadow. He had no way of knowing what that ancient temple, long before abandoned by man, truly was, but he knew it was not a place he belonged; it was neither Jungle nor Man-village. So why had they taken him there?

Tall columns, like strong, straight tree trunks but composed of rock and granite, supported a massive canopy that cast the entire area in darkness. The floor beneath his feet was cut into a series of irregular blocks, each fitted precisely with the ones beside it to create what had once been a perfectly flat surface, now pushed apart by an intruding army of vines and roots. All of it was utterly unfamiliar to Mowgli, but that was not what concerned him. It was the eyes.

The darkness itself seemed to be alive and watching his every step, for in every corner of the structure, glowing eyes stared back at him. Behind each column, around every corner, from every possible perch, hundreds upon hundreds of monkeys looked down on him. One would dart forward, grunting aggressively, then skitter back. Then another would swing down, abrupt and threatening but taking pains never to get too close. A long-tailed shape would swing silently from one shadow to the next, its eyes glued to the man-cub.

He tried not to flinch or back away. He didn't

want to show the weakness he felt inside. Shaken,
Mowgli kept walking.

At the far end of the colonnade, he reached
towering stone steps, lit from above by a sun he
could no longer see. He didn't know where the
endless stairs led, but it had to be better than where
he was. Or so he hoped.

The crumbling stairs brought Mowgli into the
center of an ancient civilization. Awe-inspiring ruins
surrounded him. Massive vine-covered archways
across from the remnants of giant statues of man and
beast confused and astounded him. He'd never seen
anything like it.

And crawling over every surface were thousands
of monkeys.

Mowgli was bigger and perhaps even stronger
than any one of them, but he had no chance against
an army. He was outnumbered and more than a little
scared. His mind swam with images of dozens of
hissing creatures descending on him in unison, claws
digging, teeth tearing, burying him under the weight
of their numbers. If they chose to attack, he was
already dead.

One of the langurs approached the man-
cub timidly, grunting and tapping at the floor,

then absentmindedly scratched his head with his foot before running away, laughing. All around Mowgli, the other monkeys picked up the laughter, screeching and banging the ground in what seemed to be some kind of game. But to Mowgli, the ranting, screaming faces could be explained only by *dewanee*, the madness. It was terrifying.

The langur who had started the hysteria stepped forward again, gesturing for the man-cub to follow him up another flight of stairs. Mowgli hesitated. Each new environment in the ancient civilization appeared to be worse than the last. What could possibly be waiting for him next?

He shuddered to think what the ranting creatures had in store for him, but as they prodded him forward, it was painfully clear that he really had no choice in the matter.

THE **KING**

THE MAN-CUB was pushed farther up the spine of the dead city.

Mowgli rose into a grand corridor illuminated by wide holes in the stone walls, passing from brief patches of light into unsettling pockets of shadow. He could still feel the eyes of hundreds of spectators on him, but they were silent and furtive now, hidden in the darkness. Clearly this was no place for laughter.

Mowgli smelled the room before he reached it, its breath the sickly sweet scent of rotting fruit mixed with the pungent smell of a beast that had not seen the river in many moons. He hesitated, fighting his gag reflex, and the monkeys behind him prodded him onward.

Stairs, tiers, platforms, and man-made plateaus

spread up and out from the center, creating a valley of stone, an unnatural arena that could easily have housed every creature Mowgli had met in his lifetime and then some. It must be some sort of great hall. But for what purpose?

The man-cub instantly spotted the source of the sweet stench: a giant pile of rotting fruit on the floor of the hall, taller than Mowgli himself and growing larger as monkey after monkey tossed more down from the skylights. Was it preparation for some sort of hibernation, like what Baloo had told him about . . . or something else?

Mowgli looked around and felt his skin crawl as he realized that all the monkeys had withdrawn to the shadows. He stood in the center of the massive hall, an ant in a cavern, alone—and yet instinct told him there was something else out there in the dark, waiting.

He wanted to flee, wanted to be anywhere but there, but he didn't dare run.

"Hello?" he called out meekly. His tiny voice echoed off the stone structures surrounding him, but no other voice answered back.

And then he saw movement in the darkness.

A gargantuan hand reached out of the shadows

and grabbed a papaya from the pile before
disappearing back into the blackness. Mowgli's
brain tried to reconcile what he had just seen. It was
clearly the weathered gray hand of a primate, but
its size was impossible. It could have picked up the
man-cub as easily as the papaya. No creature was that
big. Mowgli's racing thoughts came to a screeching
halt as a powerful, commanding voice emerged from
the shadows.

"What part of the Jungle you from?"

"Me?" Mowgli said weakly, taking a step back.

"You. Man-cub. You come from the south? The
north? What part of the Jungle?"

"South, I think," Mowgli said uncertainly. He
truly didn't know, but even if he had, he was so
unnerved by speaking to a creature he couldn't see,
couldn't fathom, that he barely knew what he was
saying.

And then the shadows moved.

Mowgli found himself frozen in place as the
thing in the darkness leaned into the light. The
man-cub's head tilted back, then farther back as the
mammoth red ape appeared before him, only his
head still in shadow. The ape was colossal in size—
gargantuan, like the mighty rhino must seem to the

mongoose. His bloated body, the result of years of gluttony and self-indulgence, more mountain than mammal, was carpeted with stringy hair that cascaded from his oversized arms to drag in the dirt below.

Mowgli felt overwhelmed with both fear and amazement. How could a creature like that even exist?

The ape's enormous form was wrapped around a mighty throne dappled with the rotting remains of a thousand meals. It was rare that he moved from that spot, and some might wonder if he even *could* move, massive as his body was. And what reason did he have to move? His legion of foot soldiers brought him everything he needed. Even now, several of the smaller langur monkeys were crawling into and out of his hair, feeding on the scraps that fell from his jaws to land in the folds of his great belly.

"Southern Jungle," the red ape said, considering it as he sucked from another handful of papaya. "The Seeonee. Beautiful. I hear. I've never been there myself." He swallowed the sticky fruit and reached for more.

"So tell me. You ever taste the pawpaw fruit down there in the Seeonee?"

"I don't think so," Mowgli murmured. He couldn't believe he was talking to a mountain. And the mountain was talking to him.

"Some people call it, what's the word . . . 'papaya.' Stolen words. I say 'pawpaw.' Goes to the sound it makes. When it tumbles to the floor."

"Okay," Mowgli answered. What else was he supposed to say? Was that why he had been taken there? To talk about fruit? What did this monster want from him?

"Try it," the ape said, holding out a papaya. Mowgli took it, but his attention was riveted to the massive hand inches from his body. This creature could swat Mowgli like a fly. The man-cub held the papaya in his hand, unable to eat it or move.

"Do you know who I am?" the creature finally asked.

"No," Mowgli answered honestly.

The mighty ape leaned toward the tiny boy and into the light, revealing his frightening face for the first time. Mowgli struggled not to recoil as he gazed on the giant staring down at him. Fleshy pouches framed a sickly gray face, its scowling mouth leading down to thick orange whiskers matted with sticky fruit. His small, closely set black eyes peered out menacingly from under his heavy brow. A hideous smile pulled back his lips to reveal jagged yellow teeth.

"I am king of the Bandar-log. Call me . . . King Louie."

THE **CLIMB**

THE FACE of the sheer cliff frowned down at the cat and the bear.

Bagheera and Baloo, out of breath, stared up from the base of the cliff that led to the kingdom of the monkeys and, without a word, began the difficult ascent.

"If you'd asked me this morning what I'd be doing today," Baloo huffed, "climbing a mountain would have been at the bottom of the list. Right below giving a rhino a tongue bath."

Bagheera, whose sharp claws and sinewy body were custom-built for climbing trees, was not equipped to scale steep cliffs. Baloo more easily sunk his claws into the dirt and rock, using his powerful upper-body strength to pull himself up, but the going was slow.

"When I was a cub, I could've done this in half the time," Baloo wheezed.

"When you were a cub, you were carrying half the weight," Bagheera said wryly.

After what seemed like days, the unlikely partners reached the peak of the cliff side. Without hesitation they plunged down the other side into the valley. They could feel in their bones that time was running out.

Crashing through the brush, they quickly made their way to the great stone doorway: the entrance to the lost city.

"I like this. I feel good about this," Baloo said with forced enthusiasm. "What's not to like?"

As if in answer, the piercing shrieks of a thousand monkeys echoed down the corridor and reverberated through the door.

"It was a rhetorical question!" Baloo yelled back at the door. Bagheera motioned for Baloo to hush and cocked his head, listening intently to the mindless screeches emanating from inside the dark structure.

"There must be hundreds of them up there," Bagheera whispered. For the first time, Baloo sensed uncertainty in the old cat. If even Bagheera was unsettled, it was serious. But Baloo knew that his man-cub needed him; that was all that mattered. It was time to step up and the bear was determined to do just that.

"I've got a plan," Baloo said.

"Why does that not fill me with confidence?" Bagheera said with a sigh.

"Trust me," Baloo said, a mischievous smile creeping across his face as he strode with cocky assurance into the darkness beyond the mysterious door.

"Famous last words," Bagheera said to himself. The old cat hoped he was wrong.

The greatest of the great apes spoke, his words slithering from his lips like snakes.

"So you are a man-cub. A man-cub who wants to live in the Jungle?"

King Louie reached out for another handful of runny papaya, stuffing his face as he held court with the small brown boy at his feet.

"How do you know that?" Mowgli asked. How did one as great as King Louie, or even as great in *size* as King Louie, know about one little man-cub?

"I got ears," the great red ape scoffed, sweeping one mighty arm to gesture at the hundreds of skittish creatures still watching from the shadows. "My ears got ears. I know all."

Mowgli doubted anyone could know everything, but clearly the king knew more about him than he knew about Louie. Mowgli could hear Bagheera in his head, reminding him; it probably wasn't a good idea to underestimate this creature.

"I know another thing about you," Louie continued, as if reading Mowgli's mind. "You need a people. To protect you."

"I have a people," Mowgli said proudly. He wasn't sure he believed that anymore, but he said it anyway.

"Who," the king laughed, "the bear?" His great gray jowls undulated like fish flapping on the shoreline as his laughter echoed off the walls of the lost city. All around him, the monkeys joined in, not understanding his words but screeching loudly as if they did.

"Where is he now?" Louie asked, gesturing around the great arena. "He can't protect you. Only I can protect you."

Protect him? From what? Was he talking about Shere Khan? Mowgli could see that King Louie and his subjects had power—that much was clear—and protection by such a group could be helpful, but something didn't feel right to him. If he was searching for his people, for his place, for his home, this was clearly not it. Home was not a place ruled by fear.

"And I will protect you," Louie offered generously. "For a price."

Mowgli squinted at the great beast and scrunched up his brow. The king wanted to make a deal: Mowgli's safety but in exchange for what, exactly?

"I don't have anything to give you," Mowgli said, shrugging. It was true.

"I think you do," Louie replied.

"What?"

The king leaned even closer to the boy. His head was bigger than Mowgli's entire body.

"Look around, Man-cub," he said. "I got everything. I have much food, endless treasure. I sit on a throne in the largest palace in the Jungle. I command a tribe too big to count. But one thing I don't have, and that's the thing you can give me."

Mowgli waited expectantly.

"The Red Flower."

THE RED FLOWER AND THE PAWPAW

MOWGLI WAS STUNNED.

The Red Flower? What made the ancient ape think Mowgli had fire? And what could he possibly want it for? Wasn't the Red Flower bad?

"I don't have that," Mowgli said.

"You're a man, aren't you?" the king grunted.

"Yeah . . ." Mowgli answered weakly.

"That's what makes you a man. You can call the Red Flower, and control it."

"They told me not to go near the Red Flower," Mowgli protested.

"You know why they tell you that?" the great red ape bellowed. "Because once you have it, you rise to the top of the food chain, brother. Nothing in all of the Jungle can stand up to the Red Flower."

Something sinister radiated from the massive creature like the Jungle heat on a blistering summer day. Mowgli didn't believe any animal could be truly evil, but the look in Louie's red-rimmed eyes made the man-cub's heart turn cold. If Mowgli had thought things were bad with Baloo and Bagheera, it was nothing compared to this. Even a close encounter with Kaa was better.

"Please," Mowgli begged. "I don't know anything about it. I just wanna go."

"*Go?*" roared the king. "Go where, Man-cub? Where will you go?"

Mowgli had no answer. He had no place to go.

"Did you know," Louie said flatly as he scooped up another handful of fruit, "there was once only a single pawpaw tree? In the whole Jungle."

Mowgli hesitated. He had expected anger or arguing, not stories.

"We were just dirt people then, the Bandar-log. Log dwellers on four legs. Till one monkey—didn't have a name—he had a notion to look up." King Louie tilted his head back to illustrate his story.

"Saw more fruit up there than he seen his entire life. Then he looked at his feet. Saw he didn't have feet, he had hands. Four hands. So he climbed, something no one had ever done before in the history of the Jungle. He . . . *evolved*."

Mowgli stood in silence. Where was Louie going with this?

"That fruit. Must have tasted delicious. May have been the sweetest thing that monkey ever put in his mouth. So he spread that seed. So more pawpaw trees would grow. And more Bandar-log would rise up, flying high. A great people who reach and rise to the top."

Mowgli nodded, listening, agreeing with the mountain of flesh in front of him. He figured that as long as King Louie was still talking, that meant the ape wasn't crushing him or eating him or doing anything else in the horrifying pictures racing through the man-cub's head.

A self-satisfied smile crept across the hideous face that loomed over Mowgli.

"There's just one thing we need to reach our full potential," whispered the king. His breath was foul. "Bring me that Red Flower and we will rule this Jungle. I will protect you and you will want for nothing ever again."

"I can't," Mowgli replied, at a loss for anything else to say.

The massive brow crushed down over the king's squinty black eyes as his mood darkened.

"You can't or you won't?" snarled Louie.

"I can't," Mowgli repeated.

"*You will!*" roared the massive ape, his foul breath blowing back the hair on Mowgli's head as he banged his fists on the ground like an angry child. The chittering creatures scavenging his body for scraps raced for safety. Louie was furious.

You never say no to a king.

THE **NEWCOMERS**

MOWGLI'S MIND RACED, desperately trying to come up with a means of escape. The fact was, he was surrounded.

Every way he turned, he found himself blocked by swarms of monkeys. Hundreds, maybe thousands, more than he had seen in his lifetime, all moving in on him, snarling at him. Even if he could find a way to get the Red Flower, the rising tide of hissing simians wasn't going to give him the chance. He wasn't leaving there alive.

"Well, well, well," sang a familiar voice from across the sea of monkeys. "As I live and breathe, is that King Louie?"

All eyes turned to the intruder. It was Baloo, standing casually in the entryway of the Great Hall.

Despite his terror, Mowgli felt a jolt of

excitement race through his body. What was that bear doing there?

The army of monkeys shrieked their disapproval, surrounding the bear in an instant. They were all on edge, on guard, protective of their great and powerful king.

"Oh, man, look at all this," Baloo continued, waltzing nonchalantly toward the center of the arena. "The opulence. The grandeur. The monkeys. The *smell*. This is so exciting. Love what you've done with the place."

"Who goes there?" rumbled Louie.

"Me?" Baloo laughed gently. "I'm nobody. I'm nothing. But *you*. Look at you. The legends do not do you justice. Man, oh, man, you are enormous, but in the best way. Look at all that—a mountain of relaxed muscle, sitting on an ancient throne."

"Seize him," the king demanded. Instantly, the hordes of monkeys were on Baloo, on his arms, his legs, his back. One moment the bear was visible, and the next he was a mass of squirming primates.

Mowgli's heart dropped. For a second he had hoped that Baloo had a plan, a scheme, something that might help them get out of there, but instead he'd only managed to get both of them in hot water.

And then Mowgli spotted a sleek shape, dark
as the shadows, slipping behind the colonnade,
emerald-green eyes glinting from the darkness.
Bagheera!

It took all Mowgli's concentration to conceal
the smile he felt inside. Bagheera would save him.
Baloo's antics, as strange as they might be, were
doing their job perfectly, distracting Louie and the
monkeys long enough for the panther to slip in
unnoticed and make his way to the man-cub.

Baloo, still amiable and upbeat, pulled a few
chittering monkeys off his head to address King
Louie.

"Hang on, hang on," he said cheerily. "You gotta
understand, I just climbed an entire mountain to
see you. Just to be in your presence. I mean, this is a
lifelong dream come true."

"Throw him off the cliff," Louie said, clearly
unmoved.

"I have no problem with that. I don't have any
problem with that," Baloo said, nodding. "I came up
here without an appointment. It was presumptuous
of me, I'll give you that. But I was hoping—and
perhaps this isn't something you're open to—but I
was hoping to be a Bandar-log."

That got everyone's attention. Louie furrowed his giant brow.

"Say what now?" the king asked. Was the bear *dewanee*—mad? He had as much sense as the waxy blossoms of the mohwa tree. How could a bear be anything but a bear?

While they stared in wonder at Baloo, Bagheera quietly led Mowgli away from the monkeys and toward the shadows. The man-cub's heart throbbed as it would after a long run with the wolf pack, but not from exertion. This time it was from a potent mixture of fear and excitement and a tiny sliver of hope that he just might survive the day.

"Hear me out," Baloo continued as the monkeys pushed and pulled and dragged him toward the cliff. "Let me finish. You guys are going places, and I *believe*. I'm a believer. Now this is weird, I know. I'm not a monkey, but I climb, I'm extremely loyal, I'm great with people—"

A high-pitched scream cut short Baloo's rambling. A lone monkey at the back of the cluster was screeching and pointing to the spot where the man-cub *used* to be. Mowgli was gone!

As the monkeys chattered angrily, excitedly, a thousand eyes swept the Great Hall and quickly spotted Bagheera and Mowgli slipping out the temple exit.

"Run, Baloo!" Bagheera called over his shoulder as they raced out of the arena. Baloo attempted to head after them but was immediately swarmed by monkeys again, covered from head to toe.

Enraged, King Louie bellowed an order to his frantic minions.

"No. One. Leaves!"

THE **ESCAPE**

MOWGLI AND BAGHEERA RAN.

They emerged into the daylight, running full speed, pushing themselves to the limit, monkeys racing after them from every possible angle.

"What about Baloo?" Mowgli yelled. If something happened to Baloo, it would be all Mowgli's fault. . . .

"He will be right behind us," Bagheera assured him. Under his breath he whispered, "I hope."

But back in the Great Hall, Baloo was making little progress toward the door. He'd had a moment of triumph—his plan had worked!—but it was short-lived. Now he was fighting off monkeys right and left. No sooner would he kick one away or hurl one across the arena than two more would take its place.

With an ear-rupturing roar, King Louie rose to his feet, his mighty arms hauling his fleshy form from the throne. Moss and lichen tore free of his backside as it lifted off the stone surface for the first time in ages. Now standing, the red ape was easily three times taller than the valiantly fighting bear he lumbered toward.

"Oh, boy," Baloo groaned. "I think this bear has overstayed his welcome."

With a herculean effort, Baloo threw his body into a spin, flinging the monkeys from his arms and legs before slamming against one of the temple walls to knock the others off his chest and broad furry back. Before they could regroup to attack again, Baloo bolted for the exit, chased by the angry echo of King Louie's rage.

"Time to go, time to go!" Baloo called as he raced into the open. Mowgli and Bagheera, already halfway down the steps of the cold lair, risked a look back to see their furry friend far behind.

"He did it," Bagheera grunted. "The lazy good-for-nothing pulled it off."

"Hurry, Baloo!" Mowgli called.

"What do you think I'm tryin' to do?" he called back.

"Climb on!" Bagheera barked, and Mowgli quickly leapt onto his back before the panther raced toward the temple exit. Mowgli knew they had to get away from that place, and fast.

A wave of monkeys poured over the temple walls as scores of others sprouted from every crevice. Swarming like bees defending the hive, they came by the hundreds from every side, quickly surrounding their prey. There were too many of them. Bagheera could see that they would never reach the exit that way.

"We will try to hold them off," Bagheera shouted, setting Mowgli down.

" 'We'?" Baloo cried, still lumbering to catch up. "Don't I get a say here?"

"Run," Bagheera ordered the man-cub. "Go!"

Mowgli hesitated, just long enough to take one last look at his friends, the only two creatures in all the Jungle who had risked their lives to save him. They were his pack.

Then the ground began to tremble, a mighty rumbling growing louder and louder. The monkeys screamed and fled the staircase.

Something big was coming.

King Louie exploded through the doorway,

his immense frame far too large for the stone archway that now lay in ruins at his feet. Dwarfing everything around him, the heaving creature loomed over the stairway, his face contorted with anger and vengeance.

"No one touches him but me," he howled, his icy gaze falling on Mowgli.

The man-cub was petrified as he stared up in horror at the living mountain of muscle swinging across the colonnade toward him at a frightening speed. It seemed impossible to Mowgli that something so big could move so fast.

"Run!" Bagheera repeated, shoving the boy down the stairs.

Mowgli ran, terror driving his heart as he sprinted into another part of the ancient temple.

Instantly, Baloo was besieged by a mass of monkeys, and without hesitation, Bagheera leapt into the fray to fend them off. Quickly, they were both engulfed, the myriad of wriggling bodies holding them back as the king bore down on his target.

Once again, Mowgli was on his own.

THE **END** OF AN **ERA**

MOWGLI RAN BLINDLY through the dark rows of columns, hidden from the sun by the heavy stone ceiling.

There were none of the familiar smells or landmarks of the Jungle to indicate direction, and in his frantic state, he couldn't remember which way he had come. But there was no time to stop and think. He was racing for his life and he knew it.

There! He spotted a bright square of daylight at the far end of the temple. It was a literal ray of hope and Mowgli made a beeline for it.

Suddenly, the ceiling erupted as King Louie's huge frame dropped, sending debris raining from above and rocking the entire structure.

Mowgli tried to gasp, but fear pressed against his chest like an elephant's foot.

"Where you going, Man-cub?" Louie snarled, his massive bulk blocking the boy's only path to escape.

Mowgli wheeled around and ran, Louie lunging to grab the fleeing boy. The man-cub darted left behind one of the great stone columns and the ape swung a gargantuan arm right through the structure, shattering the stone; chunks as big as Mowgli flew through the air as the man-cub bolted for safety.

"Stay away from me!" Mowgli cried, running wildly to keep out of reach of the grasping hands. Panic was quickly climbing his spine and clouding his judgment. He had to get out of there. He saw a stairwell and ran for it. It was far too narrow for Louie. The man-cub put on a burst of speed and leapt up the stairs a moment before the ape king's hand crashed down where Mowgli had been standing.

As he raced up the stone stairs, the wall beside Mowgli shuddered and cracked. Louie was trying to punch his way through the solid stone. The man-cub scrambled to the opposite side of the stairwell just before a second blow reduced the wall to pebbles. The giant hand scraped and clawed through the new hole, searching blindly for Mowgli, missing him by inches. He felt the bristling orange hairs that poked from the back of Louie's hand scratching across his heels as he leapt up the last step and onto the next floor.

King Louie seethed as he yanked his hand out of the hole and threw his almost impossibly long arms up to the floor above, heaving his bulk onto the landing. The boy couldn't run forever. Nothing could stop the king of the Bandar-log from getting what he desired, what he deserved, what was rightfully his.

But then the man-cub was gone. All Louie could see were the long rows of stone pillars stretching to the horizon. He knew the boy hadn't vanished. He was hiding. And he would not stay hidden for long.

"You have no one now, boy," Louie said, slowly stalking his prey through the darkened forest of stone. "I'm your only hope."

Mowgli, his back pressed tight to one of the rock columns, tried to disappear. He tried to wish himself home, back to *his* Jungle, back to the pack, to the time before the tiger had appeared at the Peace Rock. He feared he might never see *his* Jungle again, that he might spend his final moments in that strange land where he so clearly didn't belong. No one belonged there.

His eyes darted to the shadows. The great ape didn't see him yet, but if even one of his simian minions was lurking in the darkness, a single screeching scream would give away his position in a heartbeat.

"I can make it real good for you here," Louie called out, dragging his hulking frame slowly toward the next column. Then, with unexpected speed, his arms flew around the column to engulf his prey. "Or I can make it real bad. . . ."

But Mowgli wasn't there.

Fear racked Mowgli's trembling body, sweat trickling down his neck as he heard—and felt—the ape drawing ever closer to his hiding spot.

"Where else you gonna go?" Louie asked as he pushed his way past each pillar.

"I'll go back to the pack," Mowgli said. He should have stayed silent, but he felt a powerful need to show the bullying ape he was wrong. He would never stay there. "I'll go back to Akela!"

Louie turned. The boy's voice had come from the left. He was closer now.

"Akela?" Louie said calmly. "Oh, you didn't hear?"

The ape reached quickly around the next column. No man-cub.

"Shere Khan killed him," Louie said coldly.

Mowgli felt his stomach drop. It couldn't be true. The ape's words had knocked all the air from his chest.

"Must've been on account of you." Louie shook his head.

"No! You're lying!" Mowgli cried out, unable to help himself.

The great red ape cocked his head to the side. He was getting closer.

Mowgli could smell the rot in the beast's hair, and each breath carried the stench of rancid papayas, reaching out and encircling the boy.

"I wish I was, kid," the king said, feigning sympathy. "But I tell you what. Together we can stop Shere Khan. Can make him pay for what he's done."

Mowgli covered his ears and closed his eyes. He didn't want to hear any more. He was heartbroken and scared and angry; his emotions were a tumultuous river and he was caught in its swirling current.

"You and me, we get this Red Flower, we rule this Jungle," hissed the king. "And we could kill Shere Khan."

Louie stopped, standing directly behind the pillar where Mowgli was hiding. Slowly, almost imperceptibly, his great orange hand reached around the column, his fingers flexing, itching to feel the man-cub in his grasp.

Mowgli caught the movement from the corner of his eye and dove to the ground. The giant hand closed around thin air as Mowgli rolled to his feet and ran for his life. Screaming with rage, Louie tore the pillar from the stone canopy and crashed after the boy.

As Mowgli fled, pieces of the massive stone ceiling smashed to the ground around him. The great ape's fury was destroying the entire temple. It was a death trap and Mowgli had to get out. Now.

The door was too far; he wouldn't make it. But Mowgli could see an opening, a hole in the far wall facing a refuge of trees in the distance. He made a break for it.

King Louie barreled toward the boy, his limbs smashing through pillars that buckled and snapped as the temple crumbled around him.

"You belong to me, you hear that?" Louie bellowed. *"YOU BELONG TO ME!"*

There was no time to think. Mowgli leapt. He flew out the hole in the wall, an entire tree length above the Jungle floor, desperately flailing as King Louie burst through after him. The wall cracked and ruptured, but it held and the ape king found himself stuck, unable to move.

The shrill chorus of rock grinding against rock drew the ape's attention upward. A shadow fell across him. It was the temple.

The remaining columns could no longer support the massive weight of the ceiling. It was coming down. All of it. The temple collapsed and the king's reign came to an end.

THE **RUINS**

THE MONKEYS CHARGED in waves.

Screaming in mindless rage, primates leapt from every structure to provide reinforcements in the attack on Bagheera and Baloo. The two fought valiantly, but the odds were stacked against them; the sheer number of monkeys was wearing them down.

And then they heard the crash.

Bagheera turned instinctively toward the sound of an avalanche of rock and stone, unlike anything he had heard before. The massive temple would soon be no more.

"Mowgli!" Bagheera yelled, but of course no one could hear him over the terrible sound of destruction. Panic crept into his mind like a hungry jackal.

All eyes were on the crumbling tower as Baloo and the monkeys stopped fighting to watch.

"Mowgli . . ." whispered Baloo.

A mighty cloud of dust rose from the dying temple. Then the sky around them grew dark as the bones of the broken city blocked out the sun and spread toward them like a fog bank, roiling like the waters of the rain-swollen river.

The temple, the king, and the man-cub disappeared in the cloud of dust.

Screeching in fear and desperation, the monkeys abandoned their fight to scramble over the ruins in search of their king. Bagheera and Baloo were right behind them.

The field of wreckage was immense, and everywhere Bagheera looked, monkeys were frantically digging, howling, and chittering at one another in panic.

"Dig for him!" Bagheera shouted to Baloo as the bear clambered over the debris. "He may still be alive."

Baloo's powerful arms snatched up jagged chunks of hewn stone as large as wild deer and hurled them left and right as fast as his body would allow. His head darting back and forth, he desperately hoping to catch sight of the boy in the cracks between the stones.

"If anything happens to that kid, I'll never forgive myself," he panted.

"He was my responsibility," Bagheera said, leaping in beside Baloo, his mighty forepaws helping the bear push a large stone out of the way. "The blame lies with me, not you."

"But I filled his head with all those crazy ideas," Baloo moaned. "If he'd stayed with you, he would've had a nice long, safe, boring life. It's all my fault."

"No, we did this together," Bagheera said with a sigh. "If what I truly fear has truly come to pass, it is on both of us, my friend."

And then, suddenly, they heard a voice from above.

"Bagheera."

The two turned, looking up into the trees to see Mowgli standing in the high branches.

"Mowgli!" Bagheera cried with relief.

"Yes!" Baloo leapt into the air, pumping his paw toward the sky. "I knew you could do it, kid!"

"Stay there," Bagheera called, leaping across the ruins. "We'll come to you."

But as the panther and bear approached, overjoyed to find their young friend alive, they were taken aback to see he did not share their elation. He stared down at them, frozen.

"Is it true?" he asked without emotion.

"What?" Bagheera asked, confused.

"Is Akela dead?"

The question hung in the air and everything seemed to go silent. The ceaseless cries of the terrified primates, the intermittent rumblings of the still falling stones, everything faded away.

Bagheera and Baloo looked up at the man-cub somberly. They didn't have to say a word. He could read it on their faces. He felt the warmth in his body drain like water from his pouch; he had never felt so empty.

"You knew," he whispered in disbelief. "You *both* knew." Akela was dead. Because of Mowgli. And they had kept it from him.

"We were going to tell you," Bagheera started, but could not bring himself to finish.

"Kid, just hold on," Baloo added, moving cautiously toward the boy. But Mowgli backed away, his pain instantly evolving into anger. Anger at them. Anger at the world. Anger at Shere Khan.

Shere Khan. He had done this. And he would continue to consume the lives of those Mowgli cared about until . . .

A dark shadow took hold in his mind.

"Someone's gotta do something," he said firmly.

"No, Mowgli," Bagheera warned. "Don't—"

"Mowgli," tried Baloo, but it was too late.

Mowgli turned and disappeared into the trees.

Bagheera scrambled after him, but the rubble of the temple blocked his path. He'd never reach the boy in time.

Mowgli was gone.

DETERMINED

NOW MOWGLI WANTED to be on his own.

The man-cub ran from the fallen temple, from the lost city, from the Jungle, from everything he had known. It would be a long time before he stopped running.

As he raced on, his thoughts swirled like the turbulent waters beneath the waterfall, ideas and feelings bursting to the surface only to be submerged under the weight of the next churning question.

Anger wrestled with sadness inside his heart, each fighting for control. He felt betrayed by the ones he trusted. He felt abandoned by the pack that had raised him and even by Akela, who had left that world without any choice in the matter. He felt used by everyone.

Everyone seemed to have a claim on him, but

he was not their son, their friend, their savior. He did not belong to any of them, least of all to Shere Khan. He belonged only to himself. He would write his own story.

The few patches of blue sky visible through the dense foliage began to fade to dark purple as day gave way to night. To the west, a thin ribbon of orange split the darkness of land from the blackness of sky, spilling onto the tops of the tallest trees in the Jungle and crowning them with amber. It was the last gasp of the sun, but Mowgli's work was just beginning.

All through the late-night hours, the man-cub moved, sometimes running, sometimes walking, heedless of the wet leaves slapping at his body in the darkness, undeterred by the calls of restless carnivores seeking their next meals.

Finally, Mowgli came to the top of the mountainside and stared down from the same vista Baloo had shown him, his eyes reflecting the flickering orange glow that lit the night.

The Man-village.

The man-cub explored an alien world.

There were no leaves or branches underfoot to give away his position, but Mowgli watched every step nonetheless and was cautious to stay upwind. He didn't know what to expect and he did not want the occupants of the strange place to hear or smell him coming.

Unlike the monkeys' monumental city of stone, this was small, built out of many natural materials. Wood. Mud. Thatched grasses, not unlike the kind Mowgli had used to build the top cover of his shelter outside Baloo's cave.

The structures were lifted off the ground a little higher than the man-cub's waist, held up by wooden posts the size of small tree trunks or thick, sturdy branches. But for what purpose? They were not high enough to keep out predators. And they were too high to serve as dens for their young. Were they, like Louie's throne, merely to raise men above those around them? To make them appear more powerful? He did not know.

Hanging from the structures were unusual items Mowgli could not identify. They appeared to be animal skins but of every color under the sun and cut into unusual patterns. They hung on a vine—actually, a series of vines, wrapped the way *he* had wrapped vines to increase their strength when he had scaled the cliffs to get Baloo's honey. On the ground beside the structures were containers, made from what looked like dried mud, full of water. But why? The river was so close.

Each structure had an opening like the mouth of a cave but with straight edges like the monkeys' temple. Wooden structures led up to each opening, branches lashed to each other to create what looked like a series of artificial steps. *But surely these men can leap up such a short distance without this device, can't they?*

Mowgli felt torn and confused. In some ways, Bagheera was right. The man-cub did have things in common with the village people. They created tools, just like Mowgli. But in many other ways, the place seemed utterly strange to him. He could never see himself living there. Could he?

There was something special about it, so unlike the foreboding village of King Louie, but Mowgli felt like he was hunting something he couldn't see. He just couldn't wrap his mind around it, like a pangolin trying to reach the center of a nut it couldn't break.

A shout from inside the nearest hut brought the man-cub back to his senses. Instantly, he dropped and rolled into the shadows beneath the structure. Mowgli held his breath, his body motionless but tensed to run or to fight, whatever was required. He held still for several minutes, but no one came running to find him.

Mowgli rose on noiseless feet under the hut, putting his ear to the wooden boards above him. He listened carefully and could hear several voices at once, though it was no language Mowgli could understand. The Man-village was as strange to him as the sky is to the fish or the river is to the bird. It was nothing like the Jungle. What made Bagheera or anyone think this was where he belonged? The sooner he left, the better.

He slowly slipped out from under the structure, careful not to be spotted. In fact, the village appeared to be empty, at least outside. There was nothing moving but the undulating orange licks of the Red Flower.

The bright blossoms, mesmerizing in their beauty, burned at the top of tall wooden stalks. The flames danced in the reflection of the man-cub's dark eyes.

Without hesitation, he leapt up and plucked the nearest Red Flower from its garden.

Moments later, he was running back into the Jungle, his dark path lit by the writhing flame held high above his head.

FLOWER IN
THE JUNGLE

THE SCREAMS ECHOED through the trees.

A Jungle babbler, a simple-looking brown bird with an unmistakable shrill cry, was shrieking in terror as he launched into the sky. Immediately, his warning was picked up by his seven sisters and the white-headed babblers nearby. From high in their treetop perches, they had been the first to see the spot of light moving through the forest where no light should be.

Someone had brought the Red Flower into the Jungle, and the Red Flower meant death.

The terrified cries of kites soon joined in as multitudes of frightened birds took to the sky, trying to escape the inescapable.

High atop a precipice, Baloo and Bagheera searched the valleys, hoping to spot the man-cub.

"Bagheera," Baloo called. "Look."

Bagheera turned and glimpsed the tiny speck of orange moving swiftly through the trees far below. His eyes widened in horror. What Shere Khan had predicted was coming to pass.

Down below, where the man-cub ran, animals caught sight of the burning branch in the distance and scrambled in the opposite direction. They didn't see who or what was carrying it and they didn't care. Every nilgai, every bison, every buck had been raised since birth to fear the Red Flower and to flee as soon as they saw it. So flee they did.

Even Kaa, her serpentine body wrapped around the limbs of multiple trees high above the dark Jungle floor, was not immune. Her normally languid pace was gone as she unwound her endless coils and slithered quickly away from the orange death.

Mowgli broke free of the dark womb of the Jungle and into the moonlight as he entered the grasslands, still driven after the long distance he had traveled. His anger gave him strength. A desire for vengeance pushed him forward. His heart burned hotter than the fire he carried. He was determined to finish it that night.

He quickened his pace, oblivious to the bright blooms and tiny embers of fire that leapt from his torch toward the dry brush behind him.

ALERTING
THE PACK

SOMETHING WASN'T RIGHT. The Jungle was too loud.

Raksha rose from the floor of her cave, ears cocked, nose high in the air. She stepped cautiously out of the den, her tail switching nervously, Gray close at her heels as always. She sniffed the air but smelled no predator. The mad cawing of the vultures, ever present at Council Rock for the past two moons, was louder than usual. But beyond their ceaseless calls, Raksha could hear others. It seemed every bird in the Jungle was raising its voice in warning.

Soon the wolves of the pack perceived the change in the air and stepped out to investigate. There was something panicking not only the birds but all the animals of the Jungle. Their instincts were confirmed as a wild pig ran into their midst. Several of the wolves snarled, raising their hackles, ready to pounce, but the pig ignored them as it raced for its life.

"What's wrong, *Ami*?" Gray asked. "Why would a wild pig run right through our land? Isn't he scared of us anymore?"

"He is more scared of something else," Raksha said gravely.

"Check the other caves. Make sure everyone knows. Go." They hurried off.

"Everyone!" she barked. "It is not safe here. Get to the river. Now!"

Suddenly, Raksha sensed exactly what was wrong.

"The Red Flower," she said, almost growling to herself.

Fire was coming. She prayed that it did not mean what she feared it did.

The Red Flower was eating the Jungle.

Animals from throughout the Jungle converged on the river, frightened, confused, and alarmed, the flames spreading across the grasslands, moving ever closer.

Not since the Water Truce had so many varied creatures gathered together, but now it was in fear, the diplomacy of cooperation long forgotten. Snakes and mongooses slammed into one another, both racing to stay out from underfoot the bison, trampling Ikki's collection.

"My stick. My rock. My leaf," Ikki muttered, his pink nose twitching nervously.

"Is it another Truce?" The pygmy hog yawned as he joined the growing group of creatures.

"No. It's the Red Flower," the pangolin informed him somberly. "It's coming."

"It's the end for all of us," the giant squirrel said. This was bad.

One of the older rhinos turned to a nilgai beside him.

"What was it? Did you see it?"

"It's man," replied the nervous nilgai mother, looking right and left in fear. "He's come to the Jungle!"

Raksha overheard the nilgai's cry and felt her heart sink. So it was true.

"Naturally," said a sly voice, soft as a newborn's

pelt. Shere Khan crept out of the shadows. "As I predicted, the man-cub has returned."

"This is your doing," Raksha snarled at the approaching cat. "You knew he'd come back for us. You set this trap—"

With an ear-splitting roar, Shere Khan's tightly coiled muscles released and he leapt, eight hundred pounds of lean muscle and razor-sharp claws pouncing on a creature one-third his size. It all happened too fast for anyone to react. Raksha collapsed under his weight, pinned to the dirt.

"You forget to whom you speak," Shere Khan said, preparing to finish her.

"Enough!" boomed a voice from the shadows.

It was a powerful command, forceful, and every creature at the watering hole turned as Mowgli strode out of the darkness, the Red Flower a blazing bouquet in his hand. His eyes were fierce in the firelight, his breathing heavy and enraged.

"You want me?" he spat at the mighty tiger. "Here I am."

The Jungle held its breath. All eyes were on the man who had brought the Red Flower into their world. They trembled as they looked upon him, terrified.

Baloo and Bagheera emerged from the tree line at a run but came to a sudden stop when they saw the hundreds of frightened eyes reflecting the flickering light of the fire.

"Oh, no," Bagheera said quietly. "Mowgli . . ."

THE CHALLENGE

FEAR SPREAD from animal to animal.

Shere Khan slowly, deliberately stepped off Raksha.

"And so it begins," the cat snarled, his ears flat against his head.

"I'm not afraid of you," Mowgli shouted, turning on Shere Khan. "I have the Red Flower! No one has to be afraid of you anymore."

He looked at the other animals, wanting to share his moment of triumph. No one spoke, all eyes on the dancing flame. He had their attention. Every creature along the river was focused on the man-cub, but something about the way they were looking at him felt wrong.

"No," the cat said slyly. "I think they're afraid of something else now."

Mowgli hesitated, uncertain for a moment. What did the tiger mean?

Then the man-cub looked around at the animals up and down the riverbed. Every one of them was backing away from Mowgli in fear. The creatures the man-cub had grown up with were distancing themselves, taking shelter, some actually cowering behind the tiger.

"Wait, it's okay," he called to them, but it was no use. He felt hurt, broken, like they had wounded him without making a mark. Even Gray was hiding behind his injured mother.

"Gray, it's just me," he called to his brother. But Gray couldn't meet his eyes.

"I hate to be the one to say 'I told you so'. . ." Shere Khan said with a smile. "But here we are. . . ."

"Ami?" Mowgli called gently, knowing in his heart that *she* would understand her son posed no threat. But Raksha could not look at him, turning away from Mowgli, actually fearful of the boy she had raised.

Tears ran down Mowgli's face before he even knew what was happening. He felt like he was being torn apart from the inside. That wasn't what he had wanted. That wasn't what he'd gone there for. Did they really think he was someone to be feared? Did they not know him at all?

"The man-cub is now a man," Shere Khan said firmly. "And man brings destruction to the Jungle."

"That's not true," Mowgli protested through his tears. "I came to help!"

"That's not how it appears to be," Shere Khan snorted, turning in the direction from which Mowgli had come. Slowly, the boy followed his gaze.

Billowing smoke was rising over the trees. The grasslands were ablaze from his carelessly dropping embers on his way to avenge Akela. The Red Flower had blossomed.

"You came to destroy," Shere Khan snarled. "Come now, use the Red Flower. Use it on me, *like your father did*."

Mowgli stared at Shere Khan, his tawny hide marked with the poorly healed scars of his past, then looked around desperately for anyone still on his side. But no one would look at him. The Jungle had turned against him. Even Baloo looked away. Mowgli felt an ache inside that he couldn't describe. He had never felt as alone, as abandoned, as utterly different as he did at that moment.

"Bagheera?" he pleaded. "Tell them. I don't want to destroy anything. I brought the Red Flower to save them. Tell them!"

Bagheera averted his eyes, remaining silent.

"Even the one who loved you the most, he can't even see you," Shere Khan said with a sigh, shaking his head in mock sorrow. "You know what he sees? He sees the Red Flower. No more man-cub. Only *man*."

Mowgli was devastated. He didn't know what to do. He looked from the tiger to the orange glow in the distance; the fire he had started was spreading.

"That's what you are," Shere Khan growled softly. "That's all you've ever been. . . ."

"Stop it!" Mowgli shouted, but the strength had gone out of his voice, the torch no longer raised above his head like a weapon. He had to hold it with two hands; it was heavy now and too hot.

Shere Khan's fierce eyes narrowed as he stepped silently forward, moving in on the man-cub. Even with the fire, Mowgli was uncertain, his determination unraveled by the twisted words of the approaching cat.

"Now's your turn. Become *man*," snarled the tiger. "Show everyone what you really are."

Mowgli looked down at the flame in his hands, then at the reflection of the flickering fire in the river below. In a small still pool at the river's edge, he saw a sight that stole his breath from his mouth: the dark shape of man with a burning branch, bringing destruction to the heart of the Jungle.

Suddenly, his eyes burned, not from the smoke but from anger. That was not what Mowgli wanted. That was not who he was. That was not his story. Enraged, he knew instinctively what to do. It was the decision that would make or break him in the eyes of everyone he knew and, more important, in his own.

Mowgli howled as he thrust the torch into the river. "That's not me!"

Instantly, the flames on the torch disappeared with a hiss, white smoke rising into the air. Up and down the river, all the animals looked on in disbelief. Even Shere Khan was surprised, but for him it was a pleasant surprise.

"Oh, that was the stupidest thing you could do." The tiger grinned, digging his talons into the soft dirt as he moved inexorably toward his prey. "The one thing you had and you gave it up. Now you have nothing. No claws, no teeth, and no friends . . ."

Shere Khan moved in, thick ropes of muscle sliding smoothly under his scorched hide as, step by step, he drew closer to the man-cub.

There was no way Mowgli could outrun him. There was no way he could outfight him. There was nothing Mowgli could do.

STANDING
TOGETHER

DEATH HAD COME for Mowgli.

The man-cub dropped down on all fours, crouching like a wolf. He felt a jolt of fear race through his body, tensing up his muscles, priming his reflexes. He was scared, but he was not going to back down. Not now, not ever.

Shere Khan twitched noticeably. He hadn't expected a fight, but the puny man could offer only token resistance, if that. He could already taste the boy's flesh as he prepared to strike.

Mowgli planted his feet in the earth, digging deep for strength like a great tree. If he was destined to fall to Shere Khan, then so be it. He was ready. He would give the tiger his fight.

"This is the Law of the Jungle," came a voice

from the sidelines. It was Baloo, confidently stepping forward. "As old and as true as the sky."

"What is this?" Shere Khan growled, taking a cautious step back as Baloo moved toward the boy. Mowgli stared at the great bear in disbelief. *What is he doing?*

"The Wolf that keeps it may prosper, but the Wolf that breaks it will die." Bagheera's voice joined Baloo's as the panther stepped up beside the man-cub.

"You fools," spat Shere Khan, ready to take on all three of them.

Mowgli felt a surge of hope as his friends stepped forward for him. A fire ignited within Mowgli, a new light burning where there had been only pain, a Red Flower, unseen, but planted by his friends.

"Like the creeper that girdles the tree trunk," growled Raksha, lending her voice to the growing chorus, "the Law runneth over and back." She stood proudly beside those who were standing up for her son.

"Fine, rise up, all of you," Shere Khan hissed. "You want to put yourself between me and the man-cub? You want to throw your lives away for a human?"

In answer, the rest of the pack moved swiftly into place beside their brother, every Seeonee wolf joining the chant.

"For the strength of the Pack is the Wolf," they said as one, "and the strength of the Wolf is the Pack."

Shere Khan's blood boiled as he looked around and saw the animals behind him moving away, switching sides, joining the opposition. The whole Jungle was ready to stand against him.

"I will have you all in my teeth!" he roared. The tiger ran at Mowgli.

Instantly, Baloo rushed forward to meet the attack, flanked by snarling wolves.

Mowgli leapt forward but was suddenly knocked to the side and landed hard on his back, away from the fight. It was Bagheera, holding him down, his face inches from the boy's.

"You are not a wolf. Fight him your way," Bagheera said.

"I can use the trees?" Mowgli asked, quickly understanding what Bagheera meant.

"Tigers do not fight in trees." Bagheera nodded with a knowing grin.

Mowgli hugged Bagheera around his huge neck, then charged back into the Jungle.

As the man-cub raced through the foliage, his eyes searching the trees, his mind tried desperately to come up with a plan. What advantage did he have over Shere Khan?

He racked his brain as he sprinted deeper into the Jungle. What could he use to defeat a creature so much more powerful, so much more ferocious? The honey cliffs? Baloo's cave? Kaa? Nothing seemed to fit, but he had to come up with something quickly.

The man-cub was not as fast as the tiger, not as imposing as the bear, not as agile as the panther. He had lived with the wolves all his life, but he was not a wolf. Shere Khan called him a man, but he was not a man, either, not entirely. He was both. He was a man-cub. He was a man and an animal. He was different. And maybe that was his advantage.

Moving deeper into the dark, warm heart of the Jungle, Mowgli felt the air growing thicker, clouded with rising smoke. He was out of time.

THE BATTLE

BESIDE THE ROILING RIVER, the battle raged.

Baloo and Shere Khan reared up on their hind legs as they traded ferocious blows, with Gray and his brothers snapping at the tiger's exposed flanks.

Shere Khan caught Baloo under the chin with his razor-sharp claws, sending him sprawling. Bleeding profusely, the ravaged bear fell back, his vision blurring, darkness closing in around him.

Bagheera, nostrils flaring, raced across the bloodstained ground to attack.

Shere Khan lunged sideways, away from the wolves, throwing his entire weight against a rocky outcropping to knock one from his back. Nearly crushed against the rocks and momentarily stunned, the wolf would be an easy target for the savage orange-and-black beast above him.

Bright eyes flashing with fury, Bagheera struck with full force, knocking Shere Khan off his feet, and they tumbled across the ground, flailing and swiping and clawing at each other. A wolf lieutenant fearlessly leapt between the two to help, but his interference worked to Shere Khan's advantage. The tiger used his mighty hind legs, stabbing his fierce claws into the wolf and hurling him like a stone into Bagheera, knocking the panther back.

Shere Khan leapt to his feet and whirled as Raksha raced toward him, leading her grown cubs in a coordinated attack, Gray right behind them, determined to help. The frightful tiger rose up again, towering over them. Barking, snapping, snarling, they leapt onto his exposed underside, knocking him back and into the rushing waters of the river.

The great striped beast thrashed wildly, sending arcs of river water flying with each swipe of his paws. Shere Khan's left arm caught Gray behind the head, lifting him clean out of the water and hurling him halfway to shore.

The pangolin and the giant squirrel dove into the water, rushing to Gray's aid. Together, they pushed and pulled him onto dry land. The wolf pup was alive, but he would fight no more that day.

In the river, Shere Khan's focus was on Raksha, the one who had so long denied him his due. She dodged and darted through the water, inflicting damage every place she could by tooth or by claw while avoiding his powerful blows. Then she latched on to the tiger's belly and refused to let go, even as he plunged them both into the water, her dark fur disappearing in the blackness beneath the surface. She dug her claws deeper and held her breath as long as she could, only releasing when her lungs screamed for air.

Shere Khan roared savagely and lunged at Raksha. Mowgli's mother bared her teeth, ready to do as much damage as she could before the end.

Bagheera leapt onto Shere Khan from the side, knocking him away seconds before he could take Raksha's life. Together they plunged, bucking and twisting, back into the river.

With everyone else wounded or debilitated, it was down to those two longtime enemies, battling beneath the water's surface. Shere Khan relished the rematch as he wrapped his mighty arms around the panther, digging his claws into his dark haunches in a deadly embrace. With lightning speed, Bagheera raked a forepaw across the brute's neck, missing his jugular but digging in where the cat had been severely burned so many years before.

Shere Khan recoiled, his shrill scream smothered by the river water, and Bagheera broke free and launched himself to the surface.

The tiger erupted from the water like a geyser, landing powerful blows on Bagheera, rending flesh from his dark hide. The two ferocious predators slashed and splashed through the river, tumbling up onto the shoreline.

Bagheera hit the ground hard and winced in pain as one of his ribs cracked. Shere Khan sensed his opponent's injury and exploited it, slashing Bagheera across the face, opening red ribbons above and below his eye.

"You are no match for me," Shere Khan roared, his voice rumbling like thunder, his soul consumed with hatred. "I am bigger. I am faster. I am stronger. I am Shere Khan."

Bagheera snarled and pounced on his larger adversary yet again.

Shere Khan was right. He was the more formidable opponent, but Bagheera was the most tenacious adversary the tiger had ever faced. In the pit of his stomach, Bagheera felt the beginnings of fear seeping in.

Digging his claws into the wet earth beside the river, Shere Khan flung mud into the panther's eyes, blinding him, and attacked. The striped beast knocked Bagheera onto his back and quickly pinned him.

"You never should have stood up for the man-cub," the tiger howled, his lips pulled back in a snarl, flecks of saliva flying from his mouth. "And now you'll pay for it in blood."

Shere Khan stretched his hideous jaws wide, his lips pulled back to expose the deadly curve of his canines, and lunged for Bagheera's neck.

Suddenly, Shere Khan let out a high-pitched whine of surprise and pain as he felt himself being lifted into the air like a cub. It was Baloo, using all of his strength and momentum to come up and under the loathsome tiger, hurling him away from Bagheera.

"Not today," Baloo wheezed, stumbling from the effort; it had taken all he had left.

Shere Khan hit the ground hard, rolled swiftly back onto his feet, and wheeled to face his foes. One by one, he had defeated them and thrown them to the wind. Surely now they could see who truly ruled the Jungle.

But what Shere Khan rose to see was not an enemy in retreat but an army emboldened and standing together. Where only the panther, the bear, and the wolves had stood against him, now others were stepping forward.

Bison, rhinos, nilgais, and bucks joined the weary Bagheera and Baloo. Egrets, deer, wild pigs, and crocodiles stood shoulder to shoulder. The scavenging pangolin, pygmy hog, hornbill, and giant squirrel stepped forward. Even the vultures that had benefited so richly from Shere Khan's hunt had switched sides. They all stood for the man-cub, despite the fiery destruction he had brought to the Jungle, still roaring in the distance.

"This is a waste of my time," the tiger snarled spitefully, turning and running toward the Jungle. "It's the flesh of the man-cub I desire!"

Then the tiger was gone.

Baloo leaned wearily against Bagheera, clearly worried. "Is he going to be okay out there?"

Bagheera stared into the Jungle. "He's a smart kid. Don't underestimate him."

THE JUNGLE WRITHED, at the mercy of the Red Flower.

Shadows leapt from every tree as tongues of fire lapped at the stars. The eerie orange glow through the smoke looked like the sun and the night were at war with each other, the light eating the Jungle leaf by leaf, tree by tree.

Shere Khan stalked through the madness, hungry for the taste of man on his tongue.

"Where are you hiding, Man-cub?" he snarled. He would find the boy no matter how long it took, but he was in no mood to wait. The hunt was over; the story was at its end. Now was the time for blood.

Leaves fluttered down past the snarling cat and his gaze shot upward. The man-cub was darting across a branch. *Fool. The trees are no sanctuary from a tiger's rage.* Mounting a fallen limb, Shere Khan flew forward, up toward his prey.

"You can fool them; you can't fool me," Shere Khan taunted. "I'm the one who saw your future. I saw what you'll become."

Mowgli wasn't listening. He had too much on his mind and was not about to be pulled in by the tiger's cunning words again. The man-cub threw himself to the next branch, careful to keep distance between him and his deadly adversary. The dance had begun.

Beneath them, the quickly spreading fire roared over trees and brush. As Mowgli leapt to the next bending bough, dark smoke obscured his vision and choked his lungs. Shere Khan traversed the middle canopy, and he couldn't smell the man-cub over the overpowering odor of the smoke—but Mowgli couldn't smell the predator, either.

The man-cub slipped behind a large tree trunk, moving as quickly as he dared. His mind flashed to his final encounter with King Louie and he realized that once again he was being hunted by a much bigger, much more ferocious adversary and hiding from the battle. But against Louie, he had been in someone else's world, without any weapons, without any plan, without any hope.

That was no longer the case.

The tiger moved quickly, carelessly, leaping from branch to branch high above the burning Jungle floor, eager to finish it. He would have his teeth in the man-cub's throat that night if it was the last thing he ever did.

Mowgli sidestepped onto another branch and felt it give more than usual under his weight. He heard a cracking sound, louder and closer than the popping of the trees below. He looked down and saw, wrapped around the branch, creeper vines with figs growing from them. The branch was dead.

"How long did you really think you'd survive against me?"

Mowgli ducked behind the tree trunk, just out of sight, as the tiger moved past. Quickly, furtively, the boy threaded several vines together. There was no time to test his idea. He would have only one shot at it. No more childish tricks. This was for real.

"We don't have to fight," Mowgli called out loudly.

The tiger smiled. The boy's voice had given him

away. Now Shere Khan knew exactly where the man-cub was hiding.

"Did you think I'd let you grow old?" the tiger snarled, moving ever closer.

Mowgli stepped out of his hiding spot, readying himself. Just below, a ring of wild Red Flower bloomed around the base of the tree.

"I don't know why you hate me," Mowgli replied. "But I don't hate you, Shere Khan." He didn't want things to end this way. He had harbored the smallest hope that there was still a way out of it that would allow them both to survive, but there was no turning back now.

"Words are a man's weapon," Shere Khan roared. "Here, let me show you mine."

Shere Khan leapt to a lower branch mere yards from the bough where Mowgli stood. He stared the man-cub in the eyes. He was going to enjoy this.

The tiger was so focused he didn't notice the boy's feet were bound to a handmade harness of vines.

Shere Khan leapt at Mowgli, talons out, teeth bared, and landed hard on the weak branch.

With a mighty crack, the branch began to split from the trunk, an ever-growing fissure widening under the tiger's full weight. In disbelief, he looked up at the boy.

"Dead tree," Mowgli explained calmly.

And then the branch snapped entirely, giving way beneath them.

They plummeted, Shere Khan flailing at Mowgli in anger and terror. Then the vine harness snapped taut, halting Mowgli's fall.

The once mighty tiger looked back in horror as he fell into the fire below, consumed by his own blind rage.

And just like that, the tiger's story ended.

Dangling above the roaring flames, Mowgli covered his eyes with his arm, unable to look. His fear and determination, once so powerful, were both gone, replaced with sadness at the fiery sight below him.

THE UNTAMED FLOWER

ALL EYES were on the inferno that had once been the Jungle.

From the edge of the river, the animals stared anxiously into the smoky darkness with no way of knowing what was happening inside. Baloo set one of his heavy paws on Bagheera's shoulder. The old panther's eyes were cold and heartbroken.

Standing alone, away from the others, Raksha stared achingly into the burning horizon, hoping against hope that she would see her son one last time. No, not hoping. With every ounce of her being, she *willed* her son to be alive.

Something moved in the brush, walking toward them. The smaller animals stepped back, cowering behind the larger ones. Bagheera stood his ground. If it was Shere Khan, they would all pay for what they had done. Gray was the only one to move forward, stepping up beside his mother, feeding the small ember of hope inside him

A black figure, coated in soot, emerged from the smoke—coughing, exhausted, and clearly human. Mowgli fell to his knees at their feet, spent.

"Mowgli!" Raksha cried.

She rushed to him, her heart soaring, and nuzzled his head tenderly. Gray adopted a less subtle means of expression, leaping into his brother's arms and joyously licking the ash from his face. Despite his fatigue, Mowgli couldn't help laughing.

"That's my man-cub," Baloo cheered. "He did it!" Elated, he hugged Bagheera, who was too tired and relieved to resist. The old cat smiled at the sight of his man-cub, *his Mowgli*, alive.

The rest of the pack quickly mobbed Mowgli, barking and nipping and nudging him lovingly. The joy of reuniting with the brother they feared they had lost was infectious.

But the moment was fleeting for the man-cub as he turned to look back at the flames, a hellish sunset reflected against the dark clouds of an impending storm.

Shere Khan, but at what price?

"Come. We have to leave," Bagheera said gently.

"But I brought the Red Flower here. It's all my fault."

He felt no sense of victory at defeating Shere Khan, no elation at having protected the others from his rage. He felt only shame. Shame and regret.

"It's all my fault," he said again.

Before anyone could respond, the ground beneath their feet began to tremble. The rumble of breaking branches and pounding feet grew louder and the earth shook. The sound was coming from the Jungle.

Bursting out of the smoke was the matriarch of the great elephants, with her calf in tow, their silhouettes rimmed by the pulsing orange glow of the distant flames.

Everyone along the river stepped back and bowed to the mighty elephant and the calf Mowgli had saved. Bagheera knew she had never ventured to that part of the Jungle before and many of the smaller animals had never been so close to a creature of such immense size. Was she leading her family to safety or was she there for something else?

She walked up to Mowgli and stood over him. He was stunned but held his ground as she stared silently into his eyes for a long moment. She needed to let him know.

Something big was coming.

HELP FROM
ABOVE

THE JUNGLE was running out of time.

Mowgli searched the intense black eyes of the humongous creature towering over him. What was she trying to tell him?

His answer came in the reverberating chorus of a distant call. All the animals turned and looked toward the sound.

On a majestic cliff, high, high above the burning Jungle, a powerful bull elephant stood proudly, his trunk trumpeting into the air.

One by one, more elephants appeared. Five. Ten. Fifteen. Massive beasts that appeared to those watching from below to have gone mad.

The huge gray creatures were ripping trees from the ground with their tusks and trunks. Their heavy shoulders pushed mighty boulders from where they had lain for centuries. They yanked up bushes half their size by the roots and tossed them through the air.

Mowgli couldn't imagine what they were doing. Was it anger? For what he had done to the Jungle?

"Look!" Baloo was the first to notice it: a thin trickle of water. It poured over the top of the cliff where no water had ever fallen before.

Smashing headlong into trees, using their massive bodies to move mountains, the elephants were rerouting the river.

The thin trickle turned into a heavy stream and then a gushing torrent. They were making a waterfall.

The overwhelming volume of cascading river water flooded the Jungle like a tsunami, slowly but surely dousing the flames and arresting the wildfire in its tracks. White smoke replaced the black as the Jungle sent a signal into the sky. It had been saved.

The animals cheered as one.

"In all my years, I have seen a great many things in this Jungle," Bagheera said to Baloo as he stared up at the elephants in utter disbelief. "But tonight I have seen something I will never forget."

"You got that, brother," Baloo agreed.

Mowgli, dumbfounded, turned from the gushing water and billowing white smoke to look up into the eyes of the mother elephant again. He didn't know what to say. What *could* he say?

In a gesture of respect, the elephant looked to her child, then ran her trunk along the man-cub's arm. The favor was repaid.

And with that, she slowly turned, careful not to trample any of the smaller creatures celebrating below, and led her child away to rejoin their tribe.

Bagheera turned and spoke to the animals.

"Tonight I saw a boy without a people bring the entire Jungle together for the very first time."

"That was some trick, little brother," said Baloo.

As Mowgli stood silently watching the elephant and her calf recede into the distance, he knew that despite his mistakes, he had done something right.

Raksha approached him, her head bowed.

"I am sorry," she said quietly. "I'm ashamed that I . . ." She could not finish.

"I know, *Ami*," Mowgli replied.

Raksha moved close and nuzzled him. She wept, tears darkening her coat.

Mowgli threw his arms around her neck and buried his face in her warm fur.

"To me, you are not wolf. You are not man," said Raksha. "You are my son."

Mowgli looked at her, then looked around—at Gray, at Bagheera and Baloo, at all his friends in the Jungle. He didn't have a people; he had *many* peoples. And he was home.

A NEW
DAWN

A DARK SHAPE moved swiftly through the Jungle.

It bounded from ground to tree and back again, swinging through the foliage, leaping over obstacles, and flipping through the air.

Mowgli raced through the branches at top speed, using the Jungle itself to propel him faster and faster.

Bagheera tore across the Jungle right behind the boy, almost upon him. If Mowgli was intending to outrun the great cat, he would never succeed.

But Bagheera joined the boy, running with him after a different sort of prey altogether, a new batch of young wolves dashing through the Jungle in an attempt to join the Council.

"Just a few more turns," Bagheera called.

"I'm going high," Mowgli said.

"Stay low!" Bagheera ordered, but Mowgli had already grabbed a low-hanging vine and vaulted himself into the branches overhead.

"He never listens," Bagheera said with a sigh.

Mowgli released the vine, tumbled forward, and landed with one foot on the limb of a banyan tree, instinctively bending his knee as the bow flexed under his weight. As the branch recoiled, he bounced up to a higher branch on the next tree, then raced across the narrow perch before leaping into the air.

Exhilarated, the man-cub tucked and rolled, flipping down to the earth, where he landed directly in front of the young wolves, cutting them off.

The startled teen wolves skidded to a stop.

"Gotcha!" Mowgli yelled, laughing.

"Come on, Mowgli, that wasn't fair," said Gray, now almost as big as the boy. Mowgli couldn't believe how fast the pups had grown. "You cheated."

"Your enemy won't be playing by any rules," Bagheera said, coming up behind them. "And you must be prepared for attack from any side."

The other wolves looked down. The panther was right. Gray was about to protest, but he didn't get the chance, as a huge, heaving creature suddenly crashed through the dense Jungle leaves, gasping for breath.

"You guys . . . are going . . . too fast," Baloo panted between huge gulps of air.

Mowgli walked over to Gray and rubbed his head.

"You broke for the footpath when everyone else went high," Mowgli admonished.

"That's what you do," Gray protested.

"Maybe," Mowgli admitted. "But that's my path. You have to pick your own."

"Oooookay," Gray reluctantly agreed.

In the distance, the harmony of howling voices called out to them.

Bagheera, Baloo, and the man-cub escorted the young wolves back to their dens while the Wolf Council gathered as they had for centuries. Each wolf took his or her traditional place, save one, who now had a new position.

Raksha climbed proudly atop the rock that had once been Akela's post, to oversee the Council as its new leader. She threw back her head and howled, a rich, resonant cry that was quickly picked up by all those sitting around her.

The one exception was Mowgli. He slipped silently up into the tree where Bagheera was perched, laid his arm over the broad ebony shoulders of his companion, and watched the proceedings. From his new vantage point, the man-cub made eye contact with his mother. She acknowledged him with the slightest of smiles, then turned to the rest of the pack.

"Look well, wolves!" she called, and then howled powerfully into the sky once again. The rest of the pack picked up the refrain, and this time Mowgli joined in, his voice far from the weak attempts of the past. His howl was unique but mighty.

The branch beneath Mowgli and Bagheera suddenly shook. Down below, Baloo was climbing up to their perch, the tree protesting as the bear occasionally paused to scratch his side against the trunk, stumbling ever upward. Mowgli smiled.

A bear. A panther. A wolf pack. A man. He didn't know if it truly fit or not, but it didn't matter. It felt right to him. It was his story, after all. *Maybe you fit where you decide you fit,* Mowgli thought. This was where his family lived. This was where he had carved his own path. This was where he belonged.

THE END